DifFerenT

— An Izzy Palmer Novel —

DifFerenT

JANET MCLAUGHLIN

Absolute Love Publishing

Absolute Love Publishing
Different

Published by Absolute Love Publishing
USA

Cover design by Logynn Hailley

United States of America

ISBN: 978-0-9995773-2-5

By Janet McLaughlin

Haunted Echo
Fireworks
Different

Dedication

For all children who dare to be different

Praise for Different

"Being able to see the world through the eyes of someone with Tourette Syndrome is often difficult. Day in and day out we hear from families struggling with Tourette and everything that comes with it: bullying, ostracization, and intolerance. But we also hear stories of strength, bravery, and kindness. I applaud *Different* for bringing light to this misunderstood neurological condition and personifying the challenges our community overcomes while educating and encouraging compassion. The author does a great job of showing that the term 'different' can be used in many ways, and not just as a negative connotation."
- Amanda Talty, Tourette Association of America President and CEO

"*Different* is an insightful look into the life of Izzy, who faces every day with the challenges of Tourette Syndrome. The author allows you to feel the world from Izzy's perspective, creating an understanding that she is more like her classmates than different.
"As an educator for more than thirty years, it is wonderful to find a text that promotes an understanding of differences. I have had several students with Tourette Syndrome, and the availability of literature to build awareness for class was limited. This book lends itself to class discussions about what it means to be 'Different.'"
- Lora Netherland, M.ED Special Education Teacher

"Growing up, I never wanted to be 'different.' But then I realized that was just me. I learned early in life that being 'different' wasn't always a bad thing, it was just my new normal. The book *Different* helps others embrace their own challenges in hopes that everyone can be a better person in the long run. Living with Tourette Syndrome is never easy, but knowing others around you understand where you're coming from sure makes life a lot easier to manage. *Different* reminds us all to embrace our challenges and celebrate the ways we are all 'different.'"
- Brad Cohen, Educator, Author, Speaker, and Brad Cohen Tourette Foundation President

Praise for the Soul Sight Mysteries

"Calling all young people with psychic gifts–and everyone who's ever felt terribly 'different' from peers! Janet McLaughlin's *Fireworks* is a refreshing, relatable page-turner that artfully weaves the intrigue of mystery, the wonder of the paranormal, and the drama of tender friendships. I am a professional psychic medium who mentors psychic young adults. I will absolutely have them read this book so they can finally see themselves represented as regular people in regular life, using their unique gifts to navigate challenging situations. The book is engaging and fun, parent friendly, and quite accurate in its representation of paranormal gifts. Fireworks is a very welcome addition to my professional library. I wholeheartedly recommend this book!"
- **Amy Utsman, psychic medium**

"Janet McLaughlin's well-written *Fireworks* has given me a new genre to explore! Zoey, with very believable psychic powers, bestie Becca, their boyfriends and families all seamlessly mesh into a truly exciting mystery. Throw in 'the new guy' Dan, who sees auras, and you have one great page-turner. What makes it work is a well-constructed plot, terrific characters, and that special sauce of, 'Yeah, that was a really good book!'"
- **Gail Hedrick, author of "Something Stinks!" and "The Scent of Something Sneaky"**

"*Haunted Echo* is a fun exploration of the psychic and paranormal worlds that will have you hooked from the first chapter! Love, ghosts, an island ... who could want for more??"
- **Tiffany Johnson, psychic medium, as seen on A&E's Psychic Kids: Children of the Paranormal**

"A little intrigue, a little mischief, a little romance ... and a whole lot to cheer about. *Haunted Echo* is a fun and fast-paced read!"
- **Marley Gibson, author of "Radiate"**

"I love a good ghost story, no matter what age it's written for, and author Janet McLaughlin has created a great one with her new book, *Haunted Echo*. Zoey and Becca are funny and smart, the setting is spooky, and the plot keeps you guessing until the end. I couldn't put it down!"
- Penny Warner, author of the award-winning Code Busters Club series

"If you are in the mood for a little bit of spookiness and a whole lot of fun, Janet McLaughlin's *Haunted Echo* is sure to be a teen crowd-pleaser. The dialogue is witty and the story line unique. I normally shy away from stories that scare me, but this book is more mystery and less horror. I would describe it as a 'Ghost Whisperer' for teens with clean romance and a plot that will have you second-guessing where it is headed. With its simplistic writing, you'll breeze through this read in one sitting - just make sure it's not too late at night, or you might give yourself a little scare."
- Robin M. King, author of "Remembrandt"

"Get psyched for this paranormal adventure with Zoey Christopher and friends! When she's invited to go along with fellow cheerleader, Becca, to the Moretti family's Caribbean Island cottage, Zoey's psychic powers don't go 'on vacation.' In fact, they are stronger than ever. 'Tween readers will enjoy the mystery, suspense, action, adventure—and even romance—in this well-crafted story."
- Dianne Ochiltree, author of "Molly By Golly! The Legend of Molly Williams, America's First Female Firefighter" and other books for young readers

"I loved this book. So you know how a book is wonderful? When you put it down, yet you wish you could read through it without breaking. I became attached to Zoey...what a great character. She experiences troubles most teens don't with being psychic, but I love that she has this power. I can't wait to read the next! Def recommend!"
- Jodi Stone, author and illustrator of children's books with Anchor Group

Acknowledgements

Writing a book is like raising a child. It's best done with the help of family, friends, and experts in the field. Especially when that child has special needs. Or the book is about those needs.

Different is such a book. In writing it, I had to rely on lots of people for information and help. But it was family whom I needed the most. They know who they are, and I am so grateful to them for letting me be a part of their lives. I love you all more than you can know.

A huge "thank you!" to my incredible critique group, the SCBWI Skyway Writers. We've had members come and go over the years, but the core remains solid. A special thank you for helping with this book to Teddie Aggeles, Susan Banghart, Sandra Markle, and Augusta Scattergood.

Editors have a lot to do with shaping a book. Before I submitted *Different* to my publisher, I hired a professional editor, and there is none better (in my humble opinion) than Lorin Oberwerger. Thank you, Lorin, for your excellent counsel.

Of course, there wouldn't be a book available without a publisher. I was blessed to find the extraordinary Absolute Love Publishing. As their name suggests, they look for books that promote good and inspire love and kindness. I am so appreciative of their help and encouragement. Thank you to Caroline Shearer, Sarah Hackley, and Denise Thompson for seeing the value in *Different* and for your commitment to promoting it.

I'd also like to acknowledge the associations that support Tourette Syndrome research and the local and national groups that offer information and support to families dealing with children with neurological disorders. Listed below are a few of them.

Tourette Association of America
42-40 Bell Boulevard, Suite 205 Bayside, NY 11361
888-4-TOURET
https://www.tourette.org/
They also have an international page:
https://www.tourette.org/about-us/partner-network/international/

Jim Eisenreich Foundation for Children With Tourette Syndrome
Post Office Box 953
Blue Springs, MO 64013
http://www.tourettes.org/index.html

Brad Cohen Tourette Foundation, Inc.
885 Woodstock Road, Suite 430 - #354
Roswell, GA 30075
678-561-BCTF (2283)
brad@bradcohentourettefoundation.com
http://bradcohentourettefoundation.com/

TICS – Tourettes International Community of Support
https://www.facebook.com/TICS-Tourettes-International-Community-of-Support-1457581287869281/timeline/

Author's Note

"Are you psychic?" That's the question I get asked most often at interviews and school visits. It makes sense considering I've written two books about a gifted, intuitive teenager. I'm expecting, after the publication of *Different*, readers will ask "Do you have Tourette Syndrome?" since that's the neurological condition my protagonist has to deal with.

The answer to both questions is no. I write about a psychically gifted teen because the subject fascinates me. My past experience as a magazine publisher who interviewed many gifted people gave me the background information I needed to make my stories authentic. There is also a plethora of articles, books, and movies about psychic phenomenon making further research easy and fascinating.

Tourette Syndrome, on the other hand, is a lot less understood. There are few articles, books, or movies about it. So where, you might ask, did I get my insights and information?

The answer is both simple and complicated. A family member—I'll call her Madison—was diagnosed with TS when she was five years old. I watched her grow. Helped in times of crises. Loved and cried with her and her family. In one way, I was part of the experience. In another, I was on the outside, looking in.

What was going on in Madison's head when she couldn't walk down the street without stopping and touching the ground every few minutes? When she couldn't leave a room unless she flicked the light switch on and off at least three times? How did she feel when she lost control and went into a screaming rage? I could only guess.

And that's what I wanted to contribute to the world with this book. I wanted to let the world know about this neurological condition on an intimate level—what it's like to actually live with the condition.

When Madison was first diagnosed with Tourette Syndrome our first reaction was despair. What kind of future would Madison have? We read anything and everything we could to try and understand the disorder. What would life be like for her? How would she cope? How would we cope?

We found out quickly that tics are just the physical manifestation of TS. There can also be additional, or what the doctors refer to as co-morbid, conditions that come under the umbrella of the disorder as well.

The most common co-morbid disorders are ADHD and Obsessive/Compulsive Disorder (OCD). Add rage, anxiety, depression, and learning challenges to the list and one can understand the challenges of raising a child with TS, as well as the challenges the child has to face not only in the safe environment of the home but also in the (sometimes) more hostile environment of the classroom.

In *Different*, Izzy's issues mimic Madison's, because that's what I saw and what I know. Other children with Tourette Syndrome may exhibit different tics and disorders. That's the nature of TS. My hope is that in sharing this story through Izzy, children with TS and their parents will know that they're not alone.

As Madison grew, along with the challenges, we found the hope and joy that we thought we had lost. Children are resilient. Sometimes more so than their parents.

And, as Izzy comes to realize during the course of the novel, everybody has issues. Maybe she isn't so different after all.

Janet

Prologue

I was five years old the first time I tried to jump out of a moving car. All I'd wanted was some french fries from McDonald's. Mom said no, it was too near dinnertime. I started to kick the back of her seat. When that didn't work, I screamed until my throat hurt, but Dad still wouldn't stop. I was just a kid throwing a fit, right? You don't give in to that kind of behavior.

But this time was different. This time I totally lost control. Still screaming, I slipped out of my booster seat and unlocked the car door. I almost had it open by the time Mom reached back and grabbed me. I know for sure I would have jumped if she hadn't stopped me.

I'd had fits before, but nothing like that one. My parents knew something was seriously wrong. They took me to one doctor after another until they finally got a diagnosis.

Now, eight years and tons of medications later, I hardly have fits anymore. But my life is far from normal. Tourette Syndrome is not easy on anyone. Not on the person who has it, her family, or her friends. Sometimes I wish I could cut open my head and pluck out whatever it is that makes me tic, call out, or obsess about, well, most everything.

I know my parents love me. They tell me I'm special all the time. But I don't want to be special. I want to be like everybody else. I want to be normal.

CHAPTER One

"Isabella Palmer. Please come to the administration office."

I glance up at the intercom on the classroom wall, imagining my name hanging there in bright red letters, blinking: Isabella Palmer. Isabella Palmer.

At school, I mostly try to stay invisible but now everyone is staring at me. Waiting for me to do something stupid like touch my cheek to the desk. Or make a loud, grunting noise. Or shout out, "I have a doctor's appointment!" Which is true, but who cares?

Clamping my lips tight, I concentrate on *not* letting my tics take over. After I pack up my stuff, I tap, tap, tap my desk and make a quick exit, not looking at anyone except Abbie. She waves and smiles. It helps to have at least one good friend I can rely on.

When I get to the hallway, I let loose with the tics. I touch the floor, the wall, then the floor again. Next, I let out the grunt that's built up in my throat. It's kind of loud, but the hall is empty. No one's around to hear. I grunt again and revel in the squeaky sound my sneakers make on the linoleum floor as I start to walk. I rub the soles into the floor and make them squeak louder.

I feel better now, but I'm super annoyed at Mom. If she'd waited for class to be over like I'd asked her to, I could have met her at the school office and not gone through all that embarrassment. But no, she had to be early. I should have figured. She's paranoid about being on time for everything. Especially doctor's appointments.

About halfway down the corridor, I spy a guy wearing a bright yellow shirt slip into Mrs. Morgan's room. Jamie Barnes has a shirt on today that exact same color. I always notice what Jamie is wearing. I notice everything about Jamie. When he's just gotten a haircut. When he's late for class. When he looks sad. He looks sad a lot.

If it really is Jamie, what's he doing sneaking into Mrs. Morgan's classroom? I know for a fact it's empty after sixth period because I've hidden out there a couple of times after really bad tic episodes.

Gathering up some courage, I tiptoe up to the door and peek in the window. The classroom looks empty. Where did he go?

I can't stop myself. I lightly tap, tap, tap on the door. Frightened that he may have heard, I pull back, lean against the wall, and listen for footsteps. Silence. I take a chance and peek again.

Standing there, staring back at me from the other side of the glass window is Jamie Barnes! I freeze, unable to move or breathe. He doesn't move either.

"Izzy!"

I jump at the sound of my name echoing off

the empty corridor walls. When I glance down the hallway a familiar figure is standing there, waving at me. Mom.

"Hurry!" she yells. "I don't want to be late."

When I turn back to the window, Jamie is gone. Where is he? And what was he doing all that time in Mrs. Morgan's room?

Before she can yell my name again, I run to meet her. Now the squeaking sneakers that mark my progress down the hall annoy me. Can Jamie hear them? He knows where I am, but where is he? I glance back once but the hallway behind me is empty.

My heart pounds in my chest. I was face to face with Jamie! Only a pane of glass separated us. I've never been that close to him before. We've never really talked to each other. It's a one-way crush. I'm not sure he even knows who I am.

All the way to the car Mom chatters away, hardly taking a breath. She talks about how Friday traffic always seems worse than the rest of the week. About how rude it is to be late for appointments. It's when she starts talking about my meds that I tune her out. I've told Mom before how much I hate taking the medications. They make me gain weight, and they make me tired. But I've given up arguing about it. She'll just bring up the jumping-out-of-the-car thing. It's a no-win.

"Izzy, are you listening?"

"What? I mean, yeah. Lots of traffic. Good thing you're early."

Mom shakes her head. "Nice try. Your eyes were glazing over."

I shrug. "Sorry."

"It took you long enough to get down that hall. What was so interesting in that classroom?"

Before I can answer, Mom drops her purse and everything spills out, including her keys. By the time we gather everything up and get it stuffed back into her bag, she's forgotten about her question and starts in on my meds. Again. She's, like, obsessed with them.

I let my mind drift back to Jamie. Not just because he is one of the cutest guys in my class. Not just because he has the deepest, darkest brown eyes I've ever seen. Not just because he's tall and totally gorgeous. Well, okay, maybe that. Just a little. But really I'm curious about what he was doing in Mrs. Morgan's room. And why he'd risk getting in trouble doing it.

I think I'll talk to Abbie about it on Monday. Maybe she can help me figure out what's going on.

Chapter Two

Mrs. Morgan doesn't look happy today. Usually, she's smiling and cheerful, but now she's leaning against her desk, arms folded, lips clamped tight. After we're all seated and quiet, she starts pacing.

"Everyone turn to the white sideboard and tell me if you notice anything different."

Everyone looks. No one answers.

"Let me be more specific. Is anything missing?"

I notice a blank space on the otherwise totally covered board. What was there before? I can't remember. Amy Robins, who doesn't miss anything, puts up her hand.

"Yes, Amy?" Mrs. Morgan says.

"Wasn't there a circus poster in that blank spot? I remember because I don't like circuses. They creep me out."

"'Creeping out' aside, yes, there was a poster there. It was very special to me. I got it when I was a child, and I've displayed it in every classroom that I've taught in. It went missing sometime between last Friday and this morning. I just want it back. If someone in this classroom stole it, please return it to me. No questions asked."

My eyes open wide as I remember Jamie

slipping into Mrs. Morgan's empty classroom last Friday. When I glance his way, he's not looking at Mrs. Morgan. Instead, he's focusing on something on his desk, like it's the most important thing in the world. His neck and cheeks are turning redder by the minute. That had to be what he was doing Friday in Mrs. Morgan's classroom. Stealing that poster. But why? It doesn't make sense. Who would want an old circus poster anyway?

I don't want to rat on him, but I have this awful urge to raise my hand and tell Mrs. Morgan about what I saw. My arm is halfway up before I manage to pull it back. I sit on my hands, press my lips tight together, and take a deep breath through my nose. I. Will. Not. Say. Anything.

Stupid Billy Parker, who sits behind me, hits me on the back of my head with a spitball. I grab it and throw it on the floor. He laughs and whispers so only I can hear him, "Go ahead, retard. Raise your hand. Say something dumb."

A loud, grunting sound escapes from my throat. Mrs. Morgan looks my way.

I really don't want to but I can't stop myself. My arm shoots up in the air, waving like a flag on a windy day.

"Isabella Palmer," she sighs as she says my name. "Do you have something to add?"

I glance at Jamie. Now his face is white like there's no blood in him at all, and he's biting his bottom lip.

"Ummm. Sorry. No." I swallow another grunt that's begging to come out.

Mrs. Morgan looks away and stupid Billy kicks my chair and laughs! The kids sitting around us start to snicker. Mrs. Morgan walks over to us, sees the spitball on the floor, and hones in on Billy.

"That's enough!" she says. "Bullying will not be tolerated in this class."

Billy goes all wide-eyed. "I didn't do anything, Mrs. Morgan. Someone else must have thrown that."

This is not good. Billy will get even by being twice as mean to me. I wish she'd just ignore it and let it die out on its own.

Mrs. Morgan shakes her head, like she's disgusted with all of us, and walks back to her desk.

"Put your books away and take out a clean sheet of paper. I'm giving you all a pop quiz."

Everyone groans and books slam shut as Mrs. Morgan starts writing on the board.

While I wait for her to finish, I glance over at Jamie. He's staring at *me*. Heat starts to build up in my chest. It creeps up my face and onto my ears. I break out in a sweat, which just adds to my embarrassment.

Jamie narrows his eyes and frowns. I bite my lip to keep from saying his name, but I can't stop staring back.

"You have 20 minutes to finish this," says Mrs. Morgan. "Not a second more."

Some of the students complain, and I take advantage of the noise, turning my head and whispering, "Jamie stole the poster," just loud enough that it blends in with the grumbling. Now that I've said it, the tension that's built up in my body releases. I can focus on the paper in front of me.

Schoolwork is easy for me, except maybe for English. I often tic while I'm reading, which makes me lose my place and I have to start all over again. So I don't always finish, which means a lower grade, which really annoys me because I *know* the work! Mom says I should ask for extra time, but that's embarrassing. At least the teacher lets me do extra work to bring up my grade. But math is my best subject, and I know I can ace this quiz.

My mind slips back to the scene of Jamie's eyes staring at mine through Mrs. Morgan's window. I wish I could talk to him. Ask him why. Fat chance that will ever happen. He probably wishes I would just disappear.

A finger taps on my paper, and Mrs. Morgan says, "Isabella. Focus!"

I grab my pencil. "Yes, ma'am."

Before I begin, I throw the pencil in the air and catch it. Three times. Mrs. Morgan stands there, watching me. Totally mortified, I lower my head until my nose is just inches from the paper. She puts her hand on my shoulder, squeezes gently, and moves on. My body relaxes and I smile, relieved that she understands.

Just like I thought, the quiz is easy—for me, anyway—and I finish early. I peek at Jamie. He's still writing. I must have been staring for a while because now he's glaring at me with those dark brown eyes. I look away. A few minutes later, the bell rings.

Jamie stops me in the hallway. His usually perfect brown hair is messy like he's been raking his hands through it. He moves his face close to mine and whispers, "Stop staring at me in class, okay? Just—stop it!"

I swallow hard and back away. This is not how I imagined it would be when I finally got Jamie to notice me. I reach out to touch his shoulder. I don't want to do it, but I can't stop myself. Jamie swats my hand away.

"You're really strange, you know that?" He shakes his head and turns to leave.

"At least I'm not a thief!" I wasn't going to say anything, but he has no right to call me strange.

He spins around and glares.

Embarrassed by the whole scene, I look down at my feet. "Don't worry," I mumble. "I won't tell."

"You won't tell what? You don't know *anything*." The late bell rings. "Just mind your own business, okay?" Jamie turns and races down the hall.

CHAPTER Three

At lunch, Abbie and I take our usual seats across from each other at the long table. She pushes her dark black hair behind her ears, unwraps her sandwich, and sniffs it.

"Ugh. Baloney again." She takes a bite and wrinkles her nose. "I saw you and Jamie talking after Mrs. Morgan's class. What was that all about?" she asks between bites.

I look around. It's crowded and noisy. Nobody is paying attention to us. I lean forward and tell Abbie about seeing Jamie in Mrs. Morgan's room last Friday.

"I think he stole her circus poster."

Abbie's blue eyes squint at me. "Did you actually see him take it?"

"No, but it makes sense, doesn't it?"

She shrugs. "I guess. But—"

"Don't worry," I interrupt. "I'm not going to say anything. But I'd sure like to know why Jamie would want an old circus poster."

"So what are you going to do? Ask him?"

I poke, poke, poke Abbie's sandwich with my finger. She waits until I finish, then takes another bite.

"I don't know what I'm going to do," I say.

Abbie looks up. She smiles and waves to someone behind me. I turn and see a girl with long, blonde hair waving back. I've never seen her before. She walks over to Abbie and sits beside her. Abbie is all smiles, and suddenly I'm finding it hard to swallow my bite of ham and cheese sandwich.

"Hey, Hannah," Abbie says. "Glad you found us." Abbie turns to me. "This is my friend, Izzy Palmer. Izzy, this is Hannah Wells."

Hannah smiles at me. "Nice to meet you."

I nod back, still chewing on that one bite of sandwich. Who is this person, and why did Abbie have to go and include her in lunch? She knows meeting new people makes me nervous.

Abbie stares across the table at me, her eyes wide, telling me to *be nice.* "So"—she swivels her head back to Hannah—"how's it going?"

"Okay. I guess. Thanks for inviting me to lunch. First days are the toughest."

"Have you had a lot of them? First days, I mean?"

Hannah shrugs. "Enough to know I'd like this one to be my last."

I force myself to swallow. It's that or spit the mess out, and that would be totally gross. I can't stop myself from grunting really loudly, though, or poke, poke, poking Abbie in the shoulder. Hannah stares at me, her eyebrows scrunched together, her eyes narrowed. My face feels like it's on fire.

"Those're just Izzy's tics," Abbie says.

Hannah looks at Abbie like she's speaking some kind of weird language.

"It's something she does. It's no big deal."

Abbie pulls out chips from her lunch bag and changes the subject. "So how do you like Florida so far?"

That's it? All these years we've known each other and Abbie thinks it's *no big deal*? Well, it's a huge deal to me.

I stuff the rest of my food in my paper bag and wad it up. "I'm not hungry anymore." I stand up, look across the table. "Nice meeting you, *Hannah*." I leave without even saying goodbye to Abbie.

As I walk away, I hear Hannah ask, "Did I do something to make her mad?"

Not wanting to hear Abbie's answer, I run to the trash bin. Just as I toss in my garbage Abbie catches up with me.

"What is wrong with you, Izzy? You were so rude to Hannah."

"What's wrong with me? You're the one who dissed me. Like my tics are nothing. Like they haven't been a problem for me my whole life. Well, now you have a new friend. At least she won't embarrass you with her *tics*."

"Izzy, you know I didn't mean anything. I know how much they bother you. I also know you hate to talk about them. That's why I said they were no big deal."

What's gotten into me? I'm being a real jerk, but I can't stop myself. I'm jealous. And afraid. What if someday Abbie gets tired of me, and my problems?

I close my eyes and take a deep breath. Count to 10 like the doctors say to do when I'm upset. When I open them, Abbie is still standing there. Waiting. Being nice to Hannah is just Abbie being

Abbie. The do-gooder girl who takes in strays. I should know. I'm one of them.

Tears gather in my eyes, threatening to leak out. I wipe them away with my sleeve. "I'm sorry, Abbie. I guess that stuff with Jamie upset me more than I thought. Then this Hannah person comes along and"—I shrug—"I'm sorry."

Abbie shakes her head. "You've been really touchy lately."

"I know. I got some different meds to take from the doctor on Friday. It's some new stuff she wants me to try."

"I thought you hated taking medicine."

"I do."

Abbie sighs. "Well, I hope they help." She looks back at Hannah. "I better go back. I'll tell her you aren't feeling well."

"Sure." I bite my lip, fighting back the jealousy. "I think I'll go outside and get some sun."

When I step outside, black clouds are edging out the blue sky. I love Florida storms. The crack of lightning and the rumblings of thunder make a great cover for my grunts and outbursts. And right now, I need some relief.

I lean against the wall, watch, and wait. A streak of lightning lights up the sky. I count the seconds that pass before the thunder comes. Eight. Nine. Ten. When it finally arrives, I let out a howl that turns into a laugh.

That's how, a few minutes later, the cafeteria monitor finds me. Laughing at the sky. She rolls her eyes. "Isabella Palmer. How many times do I have to tell you it's dangerous to be outside during a storm?"

Without looking away, I say, "I'll be in in a minute, Mrs. Torres."

More lightning strikes, the thunder almost immediate. This time, my scream is a startled one. Loud thunder shakes the ground. I hustle after Mrs. Torres, laughing all the way.

CHAPTER Four

I freeze as I step up onto the bus. There's only one seat left. And it's next to Hannah Wells.

I clasp my lips tight and move forward, slip in beside her, and stuff my backpack under my legs.

Hannah looks at me. "You're Izzy, right? Abbie's friend."

Like she could forget the girl who grunts. I nod and stop myself just in time from tapping her shoulder. We sit there, not talking, for what seems like forever.

Finally, Hannah says, "Abbie's really nice."

I swallow a flash of jealousy. "Yeah, she is." I search my brain to fill in the awkward silence between us and remember Hannah saying something about first days being tough. "So sounds like you move around a lot."

Hannah nods. "Army brat. The longest we stayed anywhere was one year. You learn to make friends quickly. Dad says this is his last posting. If we like it here, we might actually stay."

"That's great." It comes out as a whisper.

I wish I meant it because Hannah's turning out to be pretty nice. It's hard not to like her. I know

Abbie will want to help her. She'll want to include her in everything. She'll be someone new I'll have to get used to. The real question is will she get used to me? My tics annoy most people.

"—stolen from Mr. McKendrick's class."

Hannah's last words burst through my thoughts. "Sorry, I was distracted. What did you say?"

"I said Abbie told me about the stolen poster at lunch today. Turns out, one went missing from one of my teachers, too. A Mr. McKendrick."

Mr. McKendrick teaches English. Could Jamie be in Hannah's English class? Did he steal that poster, too?

Before I can figure out a way to ask Hannah about Jamie, she grabs her backpack and stands. "This is my stop. I guess I'll see you tomorrow at lunch with Abbie?"

"Sure." Why not? People can be friends with more than one person, right? At least, I hope so.

After Hannah leaves, I slide over, breathe out hot air on the window, and print Jamie's name in the mist that forms: JAMIE. I've been wanting him to notice me for months, and now he has, but in the worst way possible. I'm pretty sure he stole that circus poster. Probably the one from Mr. McKendrick's class, too. But stealing posters makes no sense.

Ugh. I have to stop this. Get him and the stealing out of my head before I start obsessing about it.

Jamie. Stealing.

Jamie. Stealing.

Too late!

Jamie. Stealing.

"Isabella! Are you getting off or what?"

Startled, I look up. We're at my stop. The driver is staring at me—along with pretty much every other kid still on the bus. I rub out Jamie's name with my sleeve and grab my stuff.

"Sorry," I mumble.

Humiliated that the driver once again had to remind me to get off the bus, I walk down the never-ending aisle with my head down, working to hold in the grunt that's tickling my throat, begging to get out. After the bus pulls away, I let loose all the frustrations that have built up that day. Jamie angry with me. Billy bullying me. Hannah coming between Abbie and me.

Grunting I punch, punch, punch the air. Touch the ground. Punch the air again, and again. When I'm finished, I'm out of breath. Exhausted. Emotionally spent.

I glance back. Look all around. No one's there. I allow myself a moment of relief, then hitch my backpack over my shoulder and walk toward my house.

CHAPTER Five

Mom is in the laundry room folding clothes when I get home. I put my bag down and start fussing with a pile of jeans. Mom sighs and waits while I make the pile neat again. I grunt and tap, tap, tap her shoulder.

"Something on your mind, Izzy?"

"Somebody stole some posters from a couple of classrooms," I blurt out. "Mrs. Morgan was seriously angry." I grunt again, annoyed with myself. I wasn't going to tell her.

Mom raises her eyebrows.

"I think it was Jamie Barnes. I saw him in her empty classroom the other day." Man, this is even worse. I shouldn't have mentioned Jamie's name. Why can't I just keep my big mouth shut? "I didn't say anything to Mrs. Morgan. Can you please not tell anybody?"

"It's not up to me to tell, Izzy, but I think you should. Stealing is wrong, even if it's just a poster."

I don't tell her how important that poster is to Mrs. Morgan. Instead, I say, "Rat out Jamie? I couldn't do that. Besides, everybody already thinks I'm weird. I don't need to be known as 'Izzy the snitch.'"

Mom's quiet for a minute. She bites her lip and finally says, "I guess I can see your point. I'm sorry school's so tough on you, sweetheart. Hopefully, the new meds will help."

Meds! Mom is always looking for the next great cure. I know she means well, but she's not the one who has to take them. I grit my teeth and start messing with the clothes again. Mom gives me a look, so I tap, tap, tap her arm instead.

"Something else bothering you?"

Grunt. Tap, tap, tap. "There's a new girl in school. Her name is Hannah, and Abbie invited her to eat lunch with us today."

Mom starts folding the clothes again. "And?"

I blow out a breath of air. "I sat with Hannah on the bus ride home. She thinks Abbie is cool."

Mom hesitates, then says, "Abbie *is* cool."

"I know! But ..." Fighting back tears, I ask Mom the question that's been making my stomach churn since lunch. "Do you think Abbie will like Hannah better than me?"

"Ah. That's what's really bothering you." Mom takes my hands in hers. "Abbie has been your best friend since you started grade school. Why would she change now?"

I shrug and grunt at the same time.

"I wish I could make all your hurt go away, Izzy. I wish ..." Mom sighs, pushes my hair behind my ears. "How about we both take a break. You grab the basketball while I change into sneakers?"

When I hesitate, Mom bumps hips with me. "Come on. I need the exercise."

"Okay. But only because you need the exercise."

We spend the next half hour on the driveway shooting hoops. I'm terrible at it, but, like Mom knew it would, the physical distraction helps me relax and forget about Hannah. By the time we're done, my hair is wet with sweat. It might be afternoon in late January, but the sun is still blazing hot in Florida.

"Thanks, Mom." I give her a hug.

"Are you kidding? This is how I keep my girlish figure." She squeezes me extra hard. "Go wash up, and do your homework. I'll let you know when dinner is ready."

I head toward the door but stop after a few steps. "I love you, Mom."

She half-smiles. "I love you, too, sweetheart."

The way she says it doesn't sound right. So I say it again. "I love you, Mom."

Mom stops. Bites her lip. Then she says, real slow, "I love you, too, Izzy."

"No. No. Just say 'I love you, too.' Nothing else on the end."

She sighs, not always knowing what I need but knowing I'll make her keep saying it until it feels right to me. "I love you, too."

Satisfied, I give her a hug and head inside. Mom doesn't follow me. "Aren't you coming?"

"In a minute." Mom bounces the ball and tosses it in the hoop.

After I shut the door, I peek out the front window to see what she's doing. She's just standing there, the ball on the ground in front of her. She has a tissue in her hand, and she's wiping her eyes and blowing her nose.

I let the water that's welled up in my eyes slip

down my cheeks. I hate that I make her cry.

I head up the stairs to my room and promise myself I won't make her cry again. It's a lie. Home is safe. It's the only place I can really be me. I grunt out my unhappiness and pound, pound, pound my fist on the wall.

Did Mom hear me? I stop and listen. The front door opens and closes. Footsteps echo off the floor, moving toward the kitchen. Relieved, I head down the hall. First a shower, then my homework. In that order.

I walk into the bathroom, flick the light switch on. Flick it off. Flick it on again. Off. Standing there in the semi-dark, I grit my teeth and flick it on one more time.

Chapter Six

Nothing much changes during the rest of the week at school. Hannah keeps showing up every day, uninvited, at our lunch table. Okay. Uninvited by *me*. Abbie sure doesn't seem to mind.

Our mid-term scores are posted on the school's website over the weekend. I get two A's, two B's, and one C. That's pretty good news, but I hate that I can't seem to pull up that gym score. Nothing I do seems to help.

On Monday morning, when I get off the school bus, I see a flyer posted on the wallboard at the front entrance:

PLAYER NEEDED FOR THE MARJORIE KINNAN RAWLINGS MIDDLE SCHOOL GIRLS SOFTBALL TEAM. DROP INTO COACH GRANT'S OFFICE TODAY AFTER SCHOOL TO APPLY. NO EXPERIENCE NECESSARY.

I know a lot about baseball. I've grown up watching the game with my dad. It's one of the things we share together, although he's a Yankee fanatic and I like the Tampa Bay Rays. We always go to the Rays' home games when the Yankees come to town. Mom usually comes, even though she's not much of a baseball fan. She says somebody has to sit between us so we won't spend the whole night arguing over calls.

How different can softball be from baseball?

Maybe, if I make the team, it will help me bring up my gym grade. Okay, I've never played the game. And maybe I'm not the most coordinated person in the world. But it did say "no experience needed." And Abbie's already on the team. Maybe she can help me.

"Hey, daydreamer. Come on. We're going to be late." Abbie comes up to me, grabs my arm.

I grunt and tap, tap, tap Abbie on the shoulder. "Did you see that flyer?"

"What flyer?" The bell rings. "Let's talk at lunch." She races toward her homeroom.

All I think about in homeroom is trying out for the team. How many girls will show up? Can I actually make the team? When I get to my first class, though, softball flies right out of my mind.

Jamie is there, standing by his seat, looking kind of pale. He's holding his side and his face is all scrunched up like he's in pain. When he notices I'm watching him, he drops his hands to his side and slides into his seat.

I can't stop staring at him.

Jamie. Stealing.

Those two words again. He turns and glares at me. I try to look away, but my mind won't let me. Abbie comes in and stands next to me by her seat, blocking my view of Jamie. I sigh in relief.

"Hey." She puts her books down on her desk and leans against it, looking down at me. "Your face is all red. Are you feeling sick?"

"No. Just stupid."

She sits. "For what?"

I shrug. "Nothing." Then I remember the flyer. "Hey. Did you know your softball coach is looking for another player?"

"Yeah. We need at least one more to fill our roster, otherwise we can't compete."

I bite my lip. Tap, tap, tap my desk.

"What?" Abbie asks.

"I was thinking of trying out for the team."

"Really? I know you love the game, but you have—" She stops, clears her throat. "I'm sorry, Izzy. You just took me by surprise. I think it's a great idea."

"You were about to say I have Tourette Syndrome and how can I play a sport when I can't even get it together in gym, right?" I grunt. Bend over and touch the floor. Try to hide the hurt and anger.

"No. That's not it—"

Before she can finish, Mrs. Morgan comes in.

I can see Abbie trying to get my attention, but I ignore her. A little later, she passes me a note with a stick drawing of a girl holding a baseball bat with my name under it. Beside it is a sad face with a teardrop and "sorry" written under that.

It's a small thing, but it means a lot to me. The hurt goes away and my entire body relaxes. I smile and mouth, "That's okay."

Before I try out, I want to talk to Abbie to find out if her coach is the kind of person who would accept someone like me. When I tried out for the tennis team last year, I was so nervous that I twirled and touched the ground before every serve.

The coach cut me on the first day. She said she had too many players, but I knew better. I saw her rolling her eyes and shaking her head after each twirl. Dad wanted to go see her. He said something about discrimination, but I told him no. I don't want to go where I'm not wanted.

Same thing with gym. I'm pretty sure I could do better if the teacher had a little patience with me. But the class is big and time is limited. If the softball coach is like either one of them, I'm out of there.

CHAPTER Seven

"Softball? Really? When are tryouts?" Hannah pulls an apple out of her brown lunch bag, sets it aside, and grabs a bag of chips.

My stomach flips. I so wish I'd asked Abbie not to mention anything in front of Hannah. What if there's only one spot and Hannah tries out and gets it? I grunt and tap, tap, tap Abbie's shoulder.

"What?" she asks me.

"Nothing." I take a bite out of my sandwich and chew, chew, chew.

Abbie turns back to Hannah. "Do you play softball? We can use all the help we can get. Our team is pretty bad."

I swallow the food and grunt at the same time. This cannot be happening.

"I've played before on a couple of teams at different schools." Hannah glances my way. "Maybe we can go try out together this afternoon. It could be fun."

I shrug. "Sure," I manage to say though it's the last thing I want.

"How about I meet you both at Coach Grant's office?" Abbie asks. "I can introduce you to her.

She's really cool."

Hannah high fives Abbie. "That would be great." She turns to me, her hand up. I tap, tap, tap the table; grunt; manage a weak high five back. Hannah smiles. It's getting harder not to like her.

The rest of the day drags. I can't get the softball tryouts out of my mind. I'm having some serious doubts. Maybe this isn't such a great idea. In fact, maybe it's a stupid idea.

But Abbie did say that the coach was cool. And I'd love to be part of a team. Instead of *watching* baseball with my dad, I'd really love to *play* softball.

Play softball.

Play softball.

Play softball.

Ugh!

When the last bell rings, I take my time getting to my locker, still not sure if I should go to tryouts. But if I don't, I might never get those two words— play softball—out of my head. I pack away my books and make my way, slowly, to the gym. No one is there. Then I remember we're meeting at the coach's office.

When I finally get there, Coach is talking with Hannah and Abbie. I hesitate at the door.

This is stupid. I'll never make the team. She'll probably cringe when she sees me tic.

I'm about to turn and leave when Abbie spies me. "Coach Grant. This is the other girl I told you about, Izzy Palmer."

"Come on in." Coach waves to me.

I disguise a grunt, turning it into a cough and make myself *not* touch the floor. I can't seem to get my feet to move so I'm stuck, hanging onto the doorframe, looking stupid.

"I don't bite, Izzy."

I *cough* again. And stay put.

"Abbie, why don't you take Hannah out to the field and introduce her to the other players?"

After they leave, Coach sits behind her desk. "Come sit."

She waits while I struggle with the decision of staying or leaving.

Play softball.

Play softball.

"I want to play softball!" spills out of my mouth before I can stop it.

Coach nods. "Okay. That's a great goal. Now come sit, and we'll talk about it."

I force myself to let go of the doorframe and walk across the floor. When I finally sit the first thing I do is pick up a pencil from her desk, toss it in the air, and catch it three times. Now I'm on a roll and can't stop myself. I bend down and touch the floor, sit up, touch my chin to my shoulder, grunt, and pick up the pencil again. I take a breath, let it out slowly, and force myself to put the pencil down. I bow my head. The last thing I want is to see the look of disgust on her face.

"Izzy?" When I don't look up Coach says, "I don't want to make you uncomfortable, but I have to ask. Are you just nervous or is something else going on?"

I lift my head enough to peek at her face. She doesn't seem annoyed or anything. "What do you mean?"

Coach hesitates, then says, "I don't want to presume, but I had a student once who did a lot of the same things you just did. He told me he had a neurological condition. I don't remember what it's called, but I was wondering if you have a similar problem."

How do I answer this? Was she okay with that "other student"? Will knowing I have "a neurological condition" make her not want me on the team? Should I even tell her what that condition is called?

I'm not sure what to do or say. Then that awful sensation starts deep down in my belly and works its way slowly up through my throat, tickling it along the way. I swallow, but it won't stay down. I know it will eventually win, so I finally give in to the grunt. Which leads to me bending, touching the ground, punching the air—and grunting again.

Coach watches and waits for me to finish. "Do you want to talk about this?"

"Does it matter?" I ask. "I mean, if I have a problem, does that mean I can't try out?"

"No, Izzy. That's not what I mean. When I had that other student I did some research. I found out that there are athletes, entertainers, doctors—all sorts of professional people—who have neurological conditions and are successful at what they do. I see no reason you can't be, too. I just want to know where you're coming from."

"Okay." I tap, tap, tap her desk, touch my chin to my shoulder, and let loose with a grunt. Coach Grant doesn't cringe or look away. I decide to take the chance and tell her.

"So, yeah. I have Tourette Syndrome. That's what it's called." I look down at my hands. I'm holding them so tightly I can feel the nails biting into my skin. "But I don't like talking about it. I don't want to say anything to the team. I just want to try out like everybody else does."

Coach nods. "That's fine if that's the way you want to play it. So what kind of experience do you have?"

I squirm in my seat. "The flyer said no experience needed."

"You've never played?"

"No, but I know all the rules and watch a lot of baseball games."

Coach Grant's eyes catch mine. "More important to me than experience is commitment. I don't want to spend time and energy teaching someone who quits just because it gets rough. And it will get rough. With your problem, it might be even rougher." Coach hesitates, like she's watching to see if I'll look away, but I hold her stare. "If you're willing to give 100 percent, then I'm willing to give you a chance."

Relief fills my belly. I can't stop the smile from spreading across my face. "Thank you, Coach. I—I really appreciate this."

"Don't thank me yet." She stands and starts walking toward the door. "You haven't been to one of my workouts."

I'm not sure what she means, but I don't care. I'm just happy to have a chance to prove to myself that I can do this. I'm still sitting in the chair thinking about all that Coach said when I hear, "Palmer! Get your butt moving. Now!"

"Yes, Coach." I jump up and follow her out the door.

When we get outside, I allow Coach to get

a few yards ahead. Then I let out a joyful grunt, followed by touching the ground, which I turn into a somersault. When I stand, I glance around to see if anyone was watching. Luckily, they're all in the dugout, talking to each other.

Coach didn't say no. In fact, unlike the tennis coach, I think she'll give me a fair chance. I might actually get to play softball after all.

Play softball.

Play softball.

Grunt. Punch. Punch. Punch. Somersault.

Play. Softball!

CHAPTER Eight

When we get to the dugout, Coach says to take the field for warm-up. Hannah and I follow Abbie and plop down next to her on the infield.

"Why are we sitting?" I ask. "I thought this was practice."

Abbie wrinkles her nose, rolls her eyes. "You'll see. Be ready for a monster workout."

"Great," I grunt. And this time, it's not a tic.

We start with stretching and warm-up exercises, which are pretty easy though some of my muscles are a little sore by the time we're done. Just when I'm thinking this isn't so bad, Coach calls out, "Ten laps around the field!"

Ten laps? Is she serious? I grunt and start running with the team.

Little by little, I fall behind, which is embarrassing and brings on the touch-the-ground tic, which makes me fall behind even more. Abbie and Hannah fall back and check on me, but I tell them to go ahead. I don't want to hold anyone back.

I still have half a lap to go when the last girl is done. They're all sitting on the field, watching me.

Waiting for me to finish. Embarrassed, I run as fast as I can—which isn't very fast—and force myself not to bend over and touch the ground.

When I reach Abbie and Hannah, I drop down next to them and bury my face in my arms, glad that the humiliation is over. I'm still panting when Abbie leans toward me and says in a whisper, "You better catch your breath fast. We're not done."

Before I can ask what she means, Coach calls out, "Jumping jacks!"

I am so tired I don't have the energy to even tic. I force myself up and do the exercise, sort of. I clap my hands over my head, but my feet stay glued to the ground. Coach watches me but doesn't say anything. After a bazillion jumping jacks—okay, maybe just 25 of them—my legs are so shaky I can hardly stand, even though I barely moved them.

I am *so* out of shape.

It's those darn medications I have to take. They make me so tired I don't feel like doing anything physical. Plus, they make me so hungry that I want to eat all the time. All my clothes are starting to get tight on me. I hate taking them!

"Everything okay?" Startled, I look up. Coach is standing over me. "You look a little pale."

I glance up at her, shading my eyes with my hand. "I'm fine. Just not used to the exercise. I'll do better next time. I promise."

She tilts her head, studying me, then nods. "You need to get yourself a baseball cap for practice." Stepping back, she calls out, "Okay, everyone. Take your field positions. Izzy and Hannah, come with me."

We follow her to the dugout. She digs into a

long, green bag and pulls out a couple of gloves. "You can use these for now, but you'll want to get yourselves one as soon as possible."

"Thanks, Coach. I have a glove somewhere in a box at home," Hannah says.

Of course she does.

"Izzy, since you haven't played before I assume you don't have one."

I shake my head and slip on the worn, old glove. I punch, punch, punch the sweet spot, loving the way it feels on my hand. So soft and warm. I take it off, examine it. It has creases and spots where the leather is worn, and—

"Izzy." Coach's voice brings me back to the room. "I'm sending you out to right field. Hannah, you can back up Ali on second base for now. You said you've played that position before, right?"

Hannah nods.

"Okay. Go take your positions."

I walk-run to right field since my legs are still sore. Meghan, who plays center and I know from English class, throws a ball to me. It's a good pitch, and I almost catch it, but it rolls out of my glove. My toss back to her is truly pitiful. It doesn't even make it halfway.

I hobble over to it, pick it up, and throw it again. This time it almost gets to her. Meghan shakes her head and throws to Ali at second base. That's the last I see of the warm-up ball.

After a few minutes, Coach stands at home plate and calls, "Heads up, everyone."

She starts hitting balls to the different positions. One drops a few feet in front of me. I grab it and almost get it to Hannah. She scoops it up and throws it hard to the catcher. Right on target.

Will I ever be that good? A tinge of jealousy latches onto a grunt that makes its way up my throat and out of my mouth. I follow it up with a couple of grunt-coughs and hope nobody notices.

I try to stay alert for the next ball that will come my way, but the waiting is hard. I have to constantly fight the impulse to take off my glove and throw it in the air or bend down to touch the ground.

While I'm standing there trying not to tic, a bunch of guys run by the field, just on the other side of the fence. I turn and watch. The backs of their T-shirts read, "MKR Track." Trailing at the end is Jamie Barnes.

I didn't know he was on the track team.

As Jamie runs by he pulls up his shirt to wipe his face. His side is bruised. I guess that's why he was holding it in class the other day.

Jamie Barnes.

God, he's cute.

Jamie Barnes.

Jamie Barnes.

"Okay, let's change it up a bit." Coach's voice brings me back to the field. She holds the bat out toward first base. "Abbie, come hit some balls. Meghan, take the mound."

My stomach feels like it's filled with marbles and they're rolling round and round. Please don't call on me to bat, Coach. Please. Please. Please.

I sigh with relief when practice is over and I'm still in the field. This is so much harder than I thought it would be. I'm not sure I'm up to it.

In fact, I think trying out might have been a big—make that *huge*—mistake.

When I get to the dugout Coach calls me over. "That wasn't so bad for the first day was it?"

"I did awful." Punch. Punch. Punch. "I only caught one ball."

"Don't worry. You'll get better."

I hand her the glove she'd lent me, but she pushes it back at me. "No. Take it home with you for now. Use it until you get your own glove."

I reach out and poke, poke, poke Coach's arm, then throw the glove in the air and catch it three times.

Coach lifts an eyebrow. "You have something you want to ask me?"

I bite my lip, turn a grunt into a cough. "Do you really think I'll get better? I mean, I missed just about everything. I'll understand if you don't want me on the team."

Coach puts her hand on my shoulder. "You were so busy trying to impress me that you didn't notice the other newbies. None of them did well, Izzy, and they have a couple of practices under their belt." She gently taps my shoulder three times and smiles. "You're going to do just fine. Now go on or you'll miss your ride home."

Abbie and Hannah are waiting for me when I come out. "Well? How'd it go with Coach Grant?"

"Coach is cool." I grin at the memory of her tapping my shoulder, like she understood and it was no big deal.

"Yeah, she is. Come on. My mom said she'd give you and Hannah a ride home."

I glance at Hannah. So this is the way it's going

to be. No more Abbie and me. Now it's Abbie, *Hannah*, and me.

"I was thinking," Abbie says. "How about I come over after dinner and practice catching with you? Hannah, do you want to come? I'm sure my mom wouldn't mind picking you up."

Hannah nods. "Sure. Sounds like fun."

Fun for who? The two of them whipping the ball to each other while I run after all the ones I miss? I don't think so.

"Thanks, Abbie, but I have a lot to do tonight. Maybe another time."

Abbie shrugs. "Okay. Hannah, do you want to practice?"

"Sure," Hannah says. "I'm a little rusty. It's been a while since I played."

Darn. This is not turning out right. "Well," I say, "maybe I could put off some stuff until tomorrow."

"Great. I'll call you when we're done eating."

On the way to the car, I turn a touch-the-ground tic into a cartwheel. Hannah sees me and does a cartwheel, too. To my surprise, I find out that I'm much better at them than Hannah. Of course, I've been doing them for a while. Maybe there is something to this practice stuff after all.

CHAPTER Nine

Dad grabs me and swings me around when I tell him about being on the softball team. "That's so great. Izzy! As soon as dinner's over, I'll take you to a sports store and get you a glove."

"Let's go this weekend." I show him the one Coach lent me. "This one's okay for now. Tonight I want to practice catching. Abbie and Hannah are coming over."

"Okay, sure. Is it okay if I join you? You know how much I love baseball."

Seeing the joy light up his eyes makes me a little nervous. Will he expect too much from me? Dads love to play baseball and football, stuff like that, with their sons. Maybe he wishes I were a boy. One who didn't have Tourette's.

"So what do you say, Izzy?"

I look up at my dad. "Sorry. I was ... thinking of something. What did you say?"

"I said maybe we could go out for ice cream after we toss the ball around."

Ice cream! My family's answer to everything, both good and bad. "Yeah. Sure." Then I remember. "What about Abbie and Hannah?"

"We'll take them, too."

I stand there punching my glove, thinking about dads and their sons.

"Something on your mind?" Dad asks.

"Oh, it's nothing."

Dad stares me down. "Out with it, Izzy."

I hesitate, then ask, "Do you ever wish I was a boy? Dads want sons, don't they?"

Dad lifts my chin. His face has that serious look he gets sometimes. "I don't know about all dads but this one is thrilled to have a daughter."

I jab, jab, jab his shoulder. "Thanks, Dad."

He hugs me tight. "Let's get dinner over with so we can get to the important stuff."

Mom is quiet at dinner. Dad asks her what's wrong, but she says nothing, which really means something. Dad keeps at her until she gives in.

"It's all this softball talk. I don't want Izzy to get hurt again like she did with the tennis thing."

"This is different," Dad says. "This is softball, honey. Izzy knows all about the sport."

"She knew all about tennis, too. She took lessons all summer, and she was good!"

"Hey!" I say. "I'm right here."

"Sorry, sweetheart," Mom says, "but I can't help worrying."

Dad wipes his mouth with his napkin and throws it down on the plate. "For heaven's sake, Jen. She's 12 years old. She's not a baby." He looks at me. "I know you can do this, Izzy. I'll help you."

Mom stands and starts to clear the table. "You wouldn't be this enthusiastic if she wanted to be a ballerina or something. It's because it's baseball you're so excited!"

"It's softball, and no that's not the reason."

I can tell they're going to get into a shouting match if I don't stop this. I hate it when they fight over me.

"I love you, Mom." It pops out of my mouth like it always does when I'm upset around her.

Mom hesitates, sighs. "I love you, too."

She puts the plates on the counter and sits back down in her chair.

I tap, tap, tap the table. "Coach knows all about the Tourette's."

They both look at me, surprise on their faces.

"You never talk about your Tourette's," Mom says.

"I didn't bring it up. She did."

"*She* brought it up?"

"Yes. I was so nervous when I went to tryouts that I was ticking like crazy. She couldn't help but notice. She said she had a student who did a lot of what I did and he told her he had Tourette's. She said all she wants from me is to give 100 percent."

Dad looks at Mom. I'm praying he doesn't say "See!" or something stupid like that. But he doesn't. He waits for her to talk first.

"I guess you're going to do it whether I like it or not. Just be careful, okay? I don't want you getting hit in the head with a ball because you were distracted by a tic."

I want to say, "Thanks for the confidence," but I decide not to push it. My cell phone rings. "It's Abbie. She and Hannah are coming over to practice. They'll be here in a few minutes."

"Hannah? That's the new girl that Abbie likes?" Mom asks.

"Yeah. She tried out today, too."

Mom starts to collect the rest of the dishes. "And you're okay with her being around?"

"Why wouldn't she be?" Dad asks.

"It's nothing!" I'm tired of the conversation and Mom's questions. I just want to go practice. "Can we get started, Dad? Maybe you can teach me a couple of things before they get here."

Dad looks at the dirty dishes piled up on the counter. "You need help with those?"

Mom shakes her head. "No. Just go."

I know she's upset, but she's trying. "I love you, Mom."

She strokes my hair, her smile sad. "I love you, too."

CHAPTER Ten

Abbie fields a grounder from my dad and shoots it over to Hannah, who blasts it back to my dad, who gently tosses it to me. Annoyed and tired of being babied, I throw it back at him—hard. It flies high, and he has to jump to catch it.

Dad tosses the ball to Abbie and comes over to me. He puts his arm around my shoulder and walks me a short distance away. "I know you don't want special treatment, Izzy, but you're not ready for the harder thrown balls. Believe me, when you are, I'll send them your way."

I know he's right, but that doesn't make it less embarrassing. "All three of you are so good at what you do," I say. "I look like a stupid beginner. I *am* a stupid beginner."

"You don't look stupid, and they were beginners once, too." Dad nods toward Abbie and Hannah. "Everybody starts at the beginning."

"Yeah, but do they do it in front of so many people? It's embarrassing, Dad."

"I guess I can see your point. How about we practice ground balls for now. Just remember to keep your glove low to the ground. Let it touch the grass."

"Ok. I'll give it a try."

I grunt and start hitting my glove's sweet spot.

Punch. Punch. Punch.

Grunt.

Punch. Punch. Punch.

Grunt.

Dad knows that my tics get worse when I'm frustrated, so he throws some grounders to Abbie and Hannah while he waits for me to settle down.

"Ready?" he asks after a few minutes.

I nod.

I suck at fielding ground balls, too. Why did I say yes to Abbie and Hannah coming over? If it were just Dad and me, I wouldn't mind messing up so much. But this is torture.

Abbie suggests we practice batting.

"I have to go to the bathroom," I say. "You three go ahead and hit. I'll be right back." It's a lie. I just want to get away.

When I get to the bathroom I grab a towel and scream into it until my throat hurts. I can tell Abbie really likes practicing with Hannah. They probably think I'm the world's biggest klutz.

I *am* the world's biggest klutz. I just want to die. I am not going out there again.

Someone knocks on the door. Figuring it's Mom, I ignore it. The knock comes again.

"Are you okay?" It's Abbie. I'm too upset to answer. After a minute she says, "You've been gone a long time. I was worried."

I grunt. Punch, punch, punch the air. Force myself to answer. "I'm okay. I'll be right down."

"You know," Abbie says through the closed

door, "when I first started playing I couldn't catch the ball for anything. And forget about hitting it."

"I *said* I was okay!" Grunt. Punch, punch, punch.

"Izzy, please let me in."

Knowing Abbie, she'll stand out there forever, so I give in and open the door.

"What?" I ask.

"Your dad said he's had enough practice for one night. He wants to take us out for ice cream."

"You couldn't tell me that through the door?"

"Izzy, come on. Nobody cares if you can catch the ball or not right now. You just started. You'll get better with practice."

Abbie is really trying. It's not her fault I'm so horrible at softball.

"Do you really think I can get better?" I ask.

"You won't know if you don't try."

"You're my best friend. You're supposed to say, 'Yes, Izzy. I think you'll be great!'"

"Yes, Izzy. I—"

I poke, poke, poke her shoulder. "I was kidding. You're right. And I did promise Coach I wouldn't quit even if it gets really hard. Just next time we practice, please don't invite Hannah. It's too embarrassing."

Abbie shrugs. "Sure. So how about that ice cream? I'm hungry."

"Yeah. Me, too."

I don't tell her I'm always hungry. I don't mention my meds make me that way. Or that they make me tired. I don't say anything about any of that. But I think about it a lot.

Maybe if I eat less and exercise more I'll be faster on the field. Maybe I'll be able to catch more fly balls. Maybe, if I lose weight, I'll be able to slide onto a base and avoid being tagged out. Maybe I'll be able to get the bat around faster and hit the ball harder and farther.

Maybe, if I don't take those meds …

CHAPTER Eleven

The next day, my dad is sitting in his car waiting to take me home after softball practice.

"Where's Mom?" I ask. "She usually picks me up."

"I told her I'd bring you home. I took the afternoon off." He has a big smile on his face. "I have a something I want to show you. It's a surprise."

I wipe my sweaty face on the sleeve of my shirt, too tired to be excited. But I try for Dad's sake. "That's cool. Where is it?"

"Home."

"Want to give me a hint?"

"Nah. I don't want to spoil it. So how was practice?"

"Hot and exhausting. Plus, we had some serious batting practice, and I pretty much sucked."

"Watch your words, Izzy."

"Well, I did!"

"Maybe I can help you with that."

"How? Do you have some magic hit-a-homerun pixie dust or something?"

Dad laughs. "No. But I have something that

may be the next best thing."

Now I'm curious. But all my wheedling can't coax it out of him.

"You'll see" is all he says.

After we pull into the driveway, Dad tells me to leave my stuff in the car and follow him. When we get to the back corner of the house he stops me.

"Close your eyes and give me your hand. I'll lead you the rest of the way."

"Dad!" I'm feeling kind of silly.

"Shush. Let me do this."

Shrugging, I close my eyes. After a few seconds of stumbling along Dad says, "Okay. You can open your eyes now."

In front of me is a giant cage-like thing sitting on our lawn. It has screening all around it. Even across the top.

"Oh my god! What is that?"

Dad is dancing around like a little kid. "I wanted to do something special for you. Something that would give you a leg up on your learning curve. So I took the afternoon off, did some research, downloaded some videos on batting"—he turns and points to the ginormous cage—"and I bought you this batting cage."

He looks so happy and proud. And I'm so grateful. I appreciate it—I really do—until I think of Mom and the conversation at the dinner table last night.

"Is Mom okay with this?" I ask. "I mean this looks really expensive."

"Don't you worry about Mom. I'll handle her." He grabs my hand. "Come on. Let me show you the rest of it."

Dad lifts a corner of the screen and we walk inside. He's set up a baseball tee. There's also a big bucket of balls and a new bat sitting inside the cage. "I didn't buy you a glove. I want you with me for that so we can be sure it fits your hand."

"Wow!" Now I'm nervous. "What if I can't do it? What if you've spent all this money, and I mess up?"

"All I ask is that you try, Izzy. And honestly"— he takes a breath, sighs it out—"I'm doing this as much for me as for you. I've been hitting balls since I set it up. I only stopped to get you. Don't know when I've had so much fun."

His excitement is catching. "Can I try it out?" My hands are itching to hold that bat.

"Sure." Dad smiles. "Knock yourself out!"

I pick up the bat, toss it up in the air three times. Touch the ground. Put it down.

Dad waits me out. "Tell me when you're ready," he says.

"Let's just start, okay?" Truth is I'm not sure I'll ever be ready.

"Come look at this first," Dad says.

I walk over to him as he opens his iPad. We watch the video he's downloaded with tips on batting. It looks easy enough on the screen.

"Ready to give it a try?"

"I guess," I say.

Again I throw the bat in the air three times, but I only catch the first two. I miss the last toss and it slams into my foot. "Ow. Ow. Ow!" I slip down onto the ground and rock back and forth while squeezing my foot with both hands.

"Bet that hurt!" He bends down to look at my

foot. "Take off your shoe and let me check it out."

"I'm okay." I stand and walk around a bit. "It doesn't feel like anything is broken. I think it's just a bruise."

"You sure you're okay?" I nod and he hands me the bat. "How about we try hitting the ball this time."

"Not funny!"

He smiles and shrugs. "I thought it was."

I giggle. "Yeah, it was."

This time, I tighten my grip on the bat, stand next to the tee, grunt, focus, and swing. It doesn't go far, but at least I hit it.

"Good first try, Izzy," Dad says. "The more you practice the more comfortable you'll be and the better you'll get."

"You mean the less I'll tic, don't you?"

"They're pretty much one and the same, kiddo." Dad puts another ball on the tee. "Try again."

By the time I've gone through the whole bucket of balls, I'm hitting harder and farther.

"See," Dad says. "When you were fully in the moment, when you were concentrating on the ball, you hardly ticked at all."

"I didn't tic much, did I?" Grunt. "But doing it in front of you is different than doing it in front of Coach and the rest of the team."

"This is the first step. You'll get there. Ready for another bucket of balls?"

I take a deep breath. "I don't think so, Dad. I'm really tired."

Darn those meds. I've had it with feeling fat and tired. I have to do something about them. Mom and Dad would have a fit if I quit taking them.

In fact, they probably wouldn't let me stop. Not without talking to the doctor first. But she's the one who put me on them in the first place. Maybe I should—

"Hey, Izzy," Dad interrupts my thoughts. "What's going on in that head of yours?"

Startled and feeling a little guilty, I tap, tap, tap his shoulder. "Just stuff." Grunt. Touch the ground.

"Stuff, huh?" Dad lifts an eyebrow, but when I don't answer, he lets it go. "Okay. Go get your *stuff* out of the car. Dinner will be ready soon. I'll be in in a sec."

Dad walks over to the tee, adjusts its height. A big grin spreads across his face. I watch from outside the cage as he hits ball after ball. He looks so happy.

I have a feeling I won't see Dad again until Mom calls him in for dinner.

CHAPTER TwelVe

The alarm on my phone wakes me up the next morning. I'm in the bathroom, pulling my hair into a ponytail, when my stomach gurgles. That's when I remember last night's dinner.

Mom didn't talk to Dad at all. It was just, "Izzy, tell your dad this," and "Izzy, ask your dad that." Finally, I couldn't take it anymore. I told them I was going to go do my homework. I could hear them yelling at each for a long time after I left.

I take my time getting ready, not wanting to go downstairs and face Mom. I mean it wasn't my idea to buy the batting cage!

"Izzy! If you don't come down right now you won't have time for breakfast." Mom's voice echoes off the upstairs wall.

"Be right there!"

I stand in the bathroom, flicking the light switch on and off. On and off.

"Izzy!"

"Okay!" I give the light switch one more flick and head for the kitchen.

Mom pops the toast down into the toaster when I walk in and starts scooping scrambled eggs onto a plate. When the toast is ready, she puts everything in front of me. I quickly take a bite.

"Do you have practice tonight?"

I tap, tap, tap my fork on my plate. "Yeah." I hold my breath, waiting to hear if she's angry with me, too, or just my dad.

"Then make sure you eat all your eggs. You'll need all the energy you can get. You've been looking tired lately."

I let out the breath and take another bite. I guess I'm in the clear. Not so sure about Dad.

"Thanks, Mom. That was delicious." I smile at her as I scoop up the last bite.

Also on the table is a glass of orange juice. Next to it are my meds. Two little pills. One to keep me calm, and one that is supposed to help with the tics. So far, it hasn't.

Or maybe it has. How would I know? Maybe my tics would be even worse without it. Or maybe they would be the same. All I know is one—or both—makes me hungry and tired.

I pick up the pills, and, like I always do, start to put them in my mouth. But this time I stop halfway. What if I didn't take them? What would happen?

Now's my chance to find out. I pretend to take the pills, but instead I palm them. When Mom's back is turned, I slip them into the pocket of my jeans.

"You haven't forgotten anything, have you?" Mom asks.

My stomach flips over. Oh my god. She saw me sneak the pills into my pocket.

"I don't see your backpack. You usually have it

by you on the floor."

I blow out the breath I'd been holding. She didn't see me.

"I must have left it in my bedroom."

"Okay. You better hurry or you'll miss your bus."

"I love you, Mom." Even though I try to stop them, the words still pop out of my mouth. Mom will know something's up.

"I love you, too."

I stand and start walking out the kitchen, but guilt fills my belly with stones. I stop and turn as the words slip out again. "I love you, Mom."

"I love you, too." She leans against the kitchen counter. "Don't worry, sweetheart. I'm not angry with you. Dad and I had a good, long talk last night. I know I have to let you do things. Sometimes it's just hard to let go."

I nod. If I try to talk, I'll blurt out about the pills in my pocket. I feel so guilty about not telling her. But if I do, she'll make me take them.

I. Don't. Want. To!

I blink back tears. "I love you, Mom."

Mom comes over and hugs me. "I love you, too."

On the bus ride to school, the pills feel like they're getting heavier and heavier. Halfway there, I pull them out of my pocket, place them on the floor, and crush them with my shoe.

It doesn't help.

I feel guiltier than ever.

CHAPTER Thirteen

"Did you know that you can soften a baseball glove with shaving cream?" It's Monday, and I'm at lunch with Abbie and Hannah. We've been talking about the team and the upcoming scrimmage.

Hannah laughs. "I didn't know that. Pretty cool."

"Yeah, just like the cream softens a beard, it can soften the leather of a glove. At least that's what the salesman said when my dad bought me my new glove on Saturday."

"Did you try it?" Abbie asks.

"Nah. Dad bought some other kind of softening stuff from the store. I think I'll keep using the old glove Coach lent me until the new one is broken in."

"I noticed you're hitting the ball pretty good lately," Hannah says.

"I've been practicing." I glance at Abbie. She knows about the batting cage, but I asked her not to tell anyone. I'm glad she didn't tell Hannah. Truth is I was kind of testing her. She and Hannah have been pretty close lately. I wanted to see if she'd keep my secret. I'm happy she did.

Abbie's changes the subject. "So guys, did you see the notice about the eighth grade dance?"

I shake my head. Hannah says, "No. When is it?"

"Three weeks from Saturday. The team usually hangs out together. It's a lot of fun."

"I've never been to any school dances," Hannah says.

"Never?" Abbie asks.

"It didn't feel right, going I mean. I was never in any place long enough to make real friends. But if the team will be there, I think it would be cool to go."

"Me, too," I say.

"I don't know about you two, but I need a new dress," Abbie says.

It's been five days since I last took my meds. I haven't been nearly as hungry or tired. And with eating less and exercising more, I've lost some weight. I bet my one good dress will be too big for me by the time of the dance. If I can get a cool-looking dress like the girls in the magazines wear, maybe Jamie will notice me.

Jamie Barnes.

Jamie Barnes.

Jamie Barnes.

"What do you say, Izzy?" Abbie asks.

"Sorry, I was thinking of something else. What did you ask me?"

"We decided we needed to go to the mall to shop for dresses on Saturday. Are you coming?"

"Yes!"

"I'll ask my mom to take us if one of your parents can pick us up."

"It's my turn," Hannah says. "I'll ask my mom."

The two of them start talking about styles and colors, but all I can think about is the new me—and Jamie Barnes.

CHAPTER Fourteen

"You've been playing with your food all through dinner," Mom says to me. "What's bothering you?"

I toss my fork in the air and barely catch it by its prongs before it hits the plate.

"Izzy!"

"Sorry." I put the fork down, wipe my hands on my napkin. "It's a tic!"

"I know, but it's a dangerous one." Mom takes a deep breath, blows it out through her nose. I can tell she's trying not to get annoyed.

I grunt, pick up my fork, hold it tight and force myself to take a bite of food. Then I put the fork down. Very carefully.

"I love you, Mom."

"I love you, too. Okay, what's bothering you?"

"The school's having a dance for eighth graders only, and I need a new dress." I turn to Dad. "I know you spent a ton of money on all this equipment and I hate to ask you—" Grunting, I pick up the fork. Toss and catch it.

Mom closes her eyes. I'm not sure she's upset about the fork or my mentioning the money for my softball stuff. Probably both.

"What do you need, Izzy? Just ask me," Dad says.

"I need some money for a dress for the dance."

Dad doesn't answer right away. He looks at Mom.

"You tell her," she says. "You're the one spoiling her."

Dad huffs out a breath, pushes back his chair. "I'm sure you heard Mom and me arguing last week after I bought the batting cage."

I nod.

"Mom thought it was a lot to spend, even though"—he throws Mom a long stare—"even though I told her I bought it for me as much as for you. But there was the glove and the cleats, too, and well, I ended up spending a lot of money."

"So does that mean I can't get the dress?" Grunt. Tap, tap, tap.

"Not exactly," Dad says, "but there are some conditions."

"What kind of conditions?" I don't like the way this conversation is going.

"First, this is not a punishment," Dad says. "Mom just wants you to understand the value of a dollar."

"Joe!" Mom's face is starting to get red.

"I mean Mom and I want you to. So yes, you can get the dress but you'll have to pay us back by doing some chores."

Tears well up in my eyes. "This is so unfair. I didn't ask for that stupid batting cage!"

Both Mom and Dad's eyes widen with surprise. I usually don't lose my temper so quickly. And the cage is really helping me with my batting. And it was sweet of Dad to get it for me. But …

The words slip out before I can stop them. "Dad said he got it for himself as much as for me. And I don't ask for much. All I want is a stupid dress."

"Izzy!" Mom says. "I think you owe your dad an apology."

"Sorry," I mumble. I won't get a dress by making them mad.

"Are you done fussing?" Mom asks.

"I said I was sorry." I tap, tap, tap the table and grunt. I can feel the tension in my body getting tighter and tighter. "Can't you just buy me the dress? I don't have time to do chores. I have practice every day after school."

"You can help around the house on the weekend," Mom says.

Another grunt. "I'm going to the mall with Abbie and Hannah on Saturday. That's the only time I have to shop." Now my voice is rising.

"Take a breath, Izzy," Dad says. "If you don't have the dress paid off by the dance, you can work off the rest later."

I don't like this change in rules. Not one bit. I grind my teeth, get up, and kick the chair.

"Fine! But I don't think it's fair springing it on me like this."

Dad eyes narrow as he glares at me. "Izzy, if you don't calm down and show some respect to your mother and me you won't be going to that dance."

I want to yell at them that I don't care if I go to the dance. I don't care if they're mad at me. I don't care! I don't care about anything!

I bite my lip to keep from shouting at them and

head upstairs to my room. I lie down on the bed, put my face into the pillow—and scream.

CHAPTER Fifteen

Jamie has a black eye! Well, not black, really. More like purple and sore looking.

He sees me staring and turns back toward the front of the class. Red creeps up his neck all the way to the top of his head. I so want to ask him what happened, but his shoulders are all hunched up. I'm pretty sure he wants to be left alone.

How did he get that black eye, though? He must be really clumsy or something because last week I saw that bruise on his side when he ran by the softball field with the track team. And now his eye and—Oh my god! Could it be? I've heard about parents who beat their kids. I don't want to believe it, but could his dad—

"Isabella." Mrs. Morgan is standing next to me.

Uh oh. What did I do now? I look up at her. "Yes," I say, holding in a grunt.

"What is it you find so fascinating?" Her voice is low so only I can hear. "You've been distracted all morning."

This time I can't hold in the grunt. "Sorry," I say, totally embarrassed. "It's"—I grunt again. Toss my pen in the air. Catch it. Start again—"It's just a tic,"

I say softly, so only she can hear.

She nods. Whispers back, "Do you need to step out?"

I shake my head. "No, thanks. I'm fine."

But I'm not fine. Now that I'm focused on them, my tics are worse. In fact, I might explode if I don't do something, so I bounce my legs up and down under the desk. I disguise a couple of grunts as coughs. I bend over and touch the floor, then retie my shoe so it looks like I have a reason for being down there in the first place.

But I do not look at Jamie Barnes.

As soon as class is over, I rush to the bathroom and explode with a long, loud grunt. When a couple of girls come in, I go into a stall and wait for them to leave. Then I punch, punch, punch the door, touch my toes—the bathroom floor is too disgusting to touch—and grunt one more time. Now I'm ready to go to the next class.

Abbie is waiting for me outside the bathroom. "You okay?" she asks.

I shrug. "I guess."

"Come on. We're already late for class." She tugs at my arm, and we run down the empty hallway.

CHAPTER Sixteen

My clothes are starting to fit me better, even hang a little, and I'm not as hungry as I used to be. The warm-ups before practice are getting easier, too. Even though I'm still running last on the laps, I can at least keep up. And I can actually lift my feet off the ground for jumping jacks like we're supposed to do. I should have stopped taking those stupid pills months ago. No, years ago!

I can't wait to go dress shopping tomorrow, either! I'm going to get a straight, short dress like all the girls in eighth grade wear. I haven't decided what color yet. Maybe red. No—

"Izzy! Heads up!" Coach calls as she hits a high fly ball out to me in right field.

Darn. I should have started running back right away, but I didn't see the arc of the ball until it was too late. It flies over my head, beyond my reach. I glance over at Meghan. Is she laughing?

"Izzy," Abbie calls from first base. "Go get the ball."

I pull my eyes away from Meghan. What is wrong with me? Grunting I bend over, touch the ground, and run back to the fence where the ball has landed. I grab it and pitch it toward home plate where Coach is standing. It only makes it halfway, but that's a pretty good toss for me. I'm getting stronger, and my batting is much better. I just have to focus.

After practice, Coach pulls me aside.

"Everything okay?" she asks.

"Yeah. Why?"

"You seem more distracted then usual lately. Any problems at school or home?"

I grunt. Tap, tap, tap her shoulder. "Everything's fine." An awful thought pops into my mind. "You're not kicking me off the team, are you? I'll pay more attention. I promise."

Coach pulls her eyebrows together. "Whatever gave you that idea? On the contrary, I have to say I'm impressed with how far you've come in such a short time."

"Thanks, Coach!" I smile and poke, poke, poke her shoulder. "I'm trying. I practice every night with my dad. Sometimes Abbie comes over, too."

"Well, it shows. Keep it up." She starts to leave, then turns back. "By the way, not sure if Abbie told you, but everyone plays at least three innings for every game. That includes scrimmages. I'm sure by next Wednesday you'll be even stronger, but I do want you to work on focusing. You seem to get distracted out there in the field."

I swallow a grunt. I've been putting the thought of the scrimmage out of my mind as best I could. But the closer the game gets, the more real it is, and the more nervous I get so the more I tic.

I give Coach a fake smile. "Great," I say, "I'm looking forward to it."

Coach nods. "Okay. I'll see you Monday. Enjoy your weekend."

The stress starts to build as soon as I leave the dugout. Mom will definitely show up. Dad will probably leave work early and come. What if I mess up? Will they start fighting about the batting cage and all that money again?

What if I have to touch the ground and do a 360 at the plate before I can bat? Okay, so I did that for tennis, not softball. But there's always a first time. And why did I have to think of that now?

It takes all my strength not to cartwheel my way to Mom's car. Instead, I do a couple of twirls.

Ugh!

CHAPTER Seventeen

I've never shopped for a dress without Mom before. In fact, I've never shopped for anything without Mom. I grunt and tap, tap, tap Abbie's shoulder.

"Where do you want to go first?"

Abbie shrugs and looks at Hannah.

"Don't look at me," Hannah says. "This is my first dance. Besides, it's your mall. You decide."

We're standing in the middle of the department store where Mrs. Anderson dropped us off. "I guess we can check out the junior department here," Abbie says.

When we get a look at the dress prices, all of us decide we need to go somewhere else.

"Let's try this one," Abbie says when we get to a popular teen store. "I've been in here a few times. They have some pretty cool stuff."

"I've always wanted to shop here," I say. "My mom always said no."

"Why?" Hannah asks.

"She thinks the outfits look cheap. Like, in tacky. I kind of like them."

"Me, too," Hannah says. "Let's check it out."

Mom was partly right. Some of the dresses have cut-outs in places I'd rather hide. But there are some cute things, too. And the prices are good. I don't want to be working off the cost of an outfit for the rest of my life.

We all pick out a bunch of dresses and go to separate fitting rooms.

I sigh and look at the dresses hanging on the hook. I brought in six of them. Two each in different sizes. Since I started losing weight, I don't know what size I wear.

I slip on a black, A-line dress with a lace and sequin top. It's a size nine, and it hangs on me like a tent. I am so excited I tap, tap, tap on the mirror and grunt. My size nine clothes were getting snug on me when I was taking my meds.

I try the same dress on in a size seven, and it fits perfectly. I step out of the dressing room and stare at myself in the three-way mirror at the end of the hallway, not believing what I see.

Abbie comes out, and her eyes go wide. "You look awesome, Izzy. I saw that your clothes were getting a little loose on you, but I had now idea that you lost that much weight."

I can't stop the smile that takes over my whole face. "Yeah, well, I've been eating less and with all the exercise," I shrug. "I guess I did lose a lot, huh?"

Hannah steps in the hallway. "Wow. Abbie's right. You look great!"

"So do both of you," I say.

"I still have a couple more dresses to try on," Abbie says.

"Me, too!" Hannah and I say at the same time.

Laughing, we all head back to our dressing rooms.

I try on a straight, sleeveless red dress with a short, stand-up collar next. It's gorgeous. I wouldn't have dared even try on a dress like this a while ago. I can't take my eyes off the me in the mirror. I look like Abbie and Hannah. Cool. Sophisticated. *Normal.*

Both Abbie and Hannah love this one on me. I decide not to even try on the other dresses. The red dress is definitely the one. And it won't take me a year to work the cost off, either.

Abbie and Hannah both end up with black dresses, but in totally different styles. We finish shopping a lot earlier than we thought and decide to go for a treat. While Abbie and Hannah both get double-dipped ice cream cones, I settle for a low calorie smoothie. I am determined to wear this dress at the dance. I kind of like the new me.

When I get home, I show Mom the dress. She looks at the tag and her eyes go big.

"Really great price, huh?" I say. "I told you that store had some nice stuff."

"I was looking at the size, not the price," Mom says. "Since when do you wear a size seven?"

"Since I—" I almost said *since I quit taking the pills*, but stopped myself in time. I grunt, then say, "Since I started softball. Coach puts us through a lot of warm up exercises and then there's the practice games. I guess it uses up a lot of calories."

Mom looks at me closely. "I've noticed your clothes were starting to get big on you, but I had no idea you lost this much weight. You're not keeping anything from me, are you?"

The blood drains from my head, and I feel a little faint. She knows about the pills! I sit down on a kitchen chair, grunt, tap, tap, tap the table and ask "What are you talking about? Do you want me to be fat!"

Mom sits opposite me. "Of course not. And you were never fat. But I can't help worrying that you might be doing something foolish like—" Mom hesitates.

I wait. I won't admit to anything.

Finally she blurts out, "You're not throwing up your food on purpose, are you?"

I know a couple of girls who do that, but no matter how much weight I gained I never even considered it.

"Is that what you think? You don't believe that I could watch what I eat and exercise and lose weight? Thanks for trusting in me, Mom!"

"Don't go getting upset, Izzy. I just worry about you. That's what moms do."

But I am upset, and I can't keep the anger out of my voice. "Why do you always do this? You always ruin things for me. I was going to try this on for you, but now I don't want to. At least my friends were excited for me." I grab the dress and head toward the stairs.

"Izzy!" Mom calls after me. "That's not what I meant. I'm sorry. Please try it on for me."

But I don't stop. She'll just have to wait for the night of the dance to see me in it.

When I get to my room, I hang the dress in the closet and sit on my bed. After a few minutes, the anger goes away and I start to feel awful. What is wrong with me? Mom didn't do anything wrong.

She was just worrying about me. I can't stand having her upset or angry.

With a sigh, I go downstairs. When I walk into the kitchen, Mom is still sitting in the same chair, staring at the wall. She blinks and looks my way.

I go over to her and give her a hug. "I love you, Mom."

She smiles, but her face still looks sad. "I love you, too." She pulls me onto her lap and brushes hair off my forehead. We sit that way for a few minutes. "How about you show me how great you look in that awesome red dress."

I smile. "I'll be right down."

I peek over my shoulder as I leave the kitchen and watch as Mom pulls a tissue out of her pocket and pats her eyes. My heart aches as I trudge up the steps. Why does this always happen?

"I love you, Mom," I whisper. But there's no answer.

CHAPTER Eighteen

Today is the big day. The one I've been looking forward to. And the one I've been dreading. Our first scrimmage. And it's at home.

Coach is starting me. Right field. Ninth batter in the line-up.

I circle around the dugout, punching my glove and touching the ground. I even tap a few people on the shoulder. Nobody seems to notice. They're all nervous, too.

Warm-ups are over, and the coaches are talking to the umps. It feels like forever before Coach comes back and tells us to take the field.

As I trot out to right field, I glance at the bleachers. Mom and Dad are in the stands. They both wave when they see me looking. I think Mom is getting used to the idea of me playing softball. In fact, by the way she's smiling and holding Dad's hands, I'd say she's even excited.

As soon as I'm in position in right field, Meghan throws me a warm-up ball. It's way high and sails over my head and into the far end of the field. As I'm running to get it, I spot the track team jogging by.

There's Jamie, tagging along at the end again.

He doesn't notice me watching as he picks up the bottom of his shirt to wipe his face. His bruised side has faded a lot. In fact, you can hardly see it. There are still traces of the black eye, though.

"Izzy! Are you going to throw me the ball or what?" Meghan has her glove up, waiting. She's looking at me with that irritated look my teachers get sometimes.

"Sorry," I mumble as I pitch the ball to Meghan. It's a pretty good throw. She only has to move a little to catch it. All that practicing is definitely paying off.

A few minutes later, the ump calls, "Batter up."

The game is about to begin.

My legs start to shake, my stomach hurts, and I feel like I have to pee. I punch, punch, punch my glove, bend over and touch the ground, then stand and grunt really loudly—out there in right field where no one can hear me. Though I notice Mom is watching. I shake myself to get rid of any more tics. I'm as ready as I can be.

Every time a batter goes up to home plate, I hold my breath. Afraid they'll actually hit the ball my way, and I might not catch it. Yet hoping they will so I can prove to myself, and my parents, that I can do this.

Sweat drips into my eyes. Bugs nip at my arms and legs. But I don't let any of that distract me. I'm ready and focused the whole time.

Three innings pass, and not one ball comes my way.

It's now the bottom of the third inning with one out, and we're at bat. Hannah's standing at home plate. I'm on deck, waiting for my turn. It's my first at bat, and my legs are as shaky as my hands. So far there's no score. In fact, no one on our team has even had a hit yet.

I bend down and grab some dirt—to hide my touch-the ground-tic—and rub it into my hands. I wipe them on my white uniform pants, leaving two big blotches of brown on my thighs. I glance over to see if Mom is watching. She smiles, waves, and gives me a thumbs-up. Unlike my regular clothes, I guess dirty uniforms are okay.

Hannah fouls the first pitch and hits the second deep into center field. It hits the ground and bounces over the fence. A ground rule double. If I hit a grounder out of the infield between first and second, Hannah could advance to third. Maybe I'd be tagged out, but I'm okay with that.

I look at Coach. She gives me the signal to bunt. That works, too. I nod that I understand and walk up to the plate.

Lots of players have little rituals they do when they're getting reading to bat. Some swing the bat over and over while they wait for the pitcher to set. Some hold the bat in the air and wiggle their butts. So when I get to the plate and punch the air three times, bend over to touch the ground, and grunt, nobody thinks it's strange.

When the pitcher sets, I get the bat ready for a bunt. I miss it. Strike one. I check with Coach. She gives me the bunt sign again. This time I hit it, but it goes foul. Strike two. Now Coach tells me to swing away. The pitch comes and it's a beauty. Right down the middle.

My bat connects with the ball. Crack! I take off at a run, so excited I forget about everything but getting to first base safely. But it doesn't matter. It was a line drive to the pitcher, who threw the ball to the second baseman. Hannah had started to run, turned when she saw the pitcher had caught it, slipped and was tagged out.

My first time at bat, and I hit into a double play to end the inning.

I take my time walking back to the dugout. Fighting to hold back the tears. Hoping my teammates will already be on the field so I won't have to face them. Coach sees me and calls me over. I figure she's going to yell or something. I stand in front of her, punching my glove and grunting.

"Shake it off, Izzy," Coach says. "You aren't the first to hit into a double play, and you won't be the last."

"But—"

"No buts. Anyway, this is a scrimmage, not the World Series. Now go out there and focus. A lefty is coming up to bat. You just may get some action."

"I thought I was only playing three innings."

"I said everyone plays *at least* three innings. You're doing just fine out there. Now hurry before I change my mind."

"Yes, Coach." As I'm leaving the dugout I turn. She's watching me. "Thanks," I say.

She nods her head toward right field. "Remember. Focus."

CHAPTER Nineteen

I stop and touch the ground twice while running to my position. When I pass Abbie, she calls to me, "I've hit into double plays lots."

I nod, but I figure she's saying that to make me feel better. It doesn't.

Let it go, I tell myself. Just focus on the game. I grunt a few times, bend over, and touch the ground. By the time I stand up, the lefty is walking to the plate.

Focus, Izzy. Focus.

The batter swings away at the first pitch. It a high fly ball, and it's sailing my way, dropping between the second baseman and me. I'm the closest, and I take off at a run. It's just a few feet away when I dive, my glove hand stretched to its limit. The ball tips the edge of the glove and rolls a little to the right. I grab it, jump up, and throw a perfect line drive to second. She catches it, and the lefty stays on first. She's not out, but at least we held her to a single.

I look at Coach. She nods her head. I take a deep breath and blow it out. I did the best I could. I have to be happy with that.

Coach keeps me in for most of the game. No more balls come my way for the next two innings. At my next at bat I get a walk. But there are already two outs, and the next batter hits an infield fly to end the inning.

The final score is 4 to 2. We lose, but not by much.

Coach calls us in for a quick meeting. As I'm walking toward the dugout, I see a guy under the bleachers, looking my way. I bend to touch the ground. When I stand up, the guy is gone.

"Izzy!" Abbie calls. "Coach is waiting for you."

"Coming!"

That shadow under the bleachers. Was it Jamie? A tingle runs up my spine. Stop it, Izzy. Jamie doesn't want anything to do with you. You're living in a dream world if you think...

"Izzy!"

"Okay! I'm coming!"

"Is there a problem?" Coach asks when I get to the dugout.

I shake my head. "Sorry, Coach. I thought I saw someone I know."

"When you're here, it's team first, friends second." She looks around. "That goes for all of you. Don't get distracted by the people in the stands. Focus on the game, and you'll do fine." She puts her hands on her hips. "So. Not a bad game for an opening scrimmage."

"We lost!" Meghan says it, but we're all thinking it.

"You did your best, and that's all I ask of you. Of course, your best now is not what your best will be by the end of the season. I'm going to work you all hard, especially on the basics. That's where the game is won or lost. Now"—she tilts her head toward the exit—"go home and relax. Tomorrow's practice will be a tough one. Get a good night's sleep. You're going to need it!"

Mom and Dad are waiting for me outside the dugout. Dad puts his arm around me as we walk to the car.

"I played awful," I say.

"What are you talking about?" Dad stops and tilts my face up with his fingers. "You were totally in that game, ready for anything that came to you. My eyes were on you the whole time. You hardly ticked at all. I was so proud of you."

"What? For not ticking?"

Dad laughs. "No." He pauses. "Well, in a way, yes. You were so focused, Izzy. You didn't let your Tourette's stop you."

Mom comes up behind me and puts her arms around me. "I'm starved. How about we go out for a bite to eat? You can pick the restaurant, Izzy."

I'm not as hungry as I usually am, but playing ball is a lot of work and my stomach gurgles at the thought of food.

"How about Mexican?" I say.

"Mexican it is." Dad opens the doors for Mom and me to get in.

I'm halfway through eating my burrito, when I put it down. I can't eat any more of it. My stomach aches from thoughts about the double play I hit into. Those two words, *double play*, run in circles through my brain.

"Not hungry?" Mom asks. "You usually eat the whole meal and ask for dessert."

I shrug.

Dad glances at Mom. "I never like to eat after exercising either."

I stand up. "Can I be excused?"

"Are you feeling okay?" Mom asks.

"Yeah. I'm just tired."

When I come out of the bathroom, Dad is paying the bill.

"Double play!" It pops out of my mouth before I can stop it.

"What's that, sweetheart?" Mom asks.

"Nothing." But the two words haunt me for the rest of the night.

CHaPTeR Twenty

At the next practice, Coach is harder on us than ever, if that's possible. All we do is practice drills. And she keeps us an extra half-hour.

"Do you think your mom could give me a ride home?" I ask Abbie. "My mom has a meeting. She said to take the bus home, but I missed it because of the late practice."

She doesn't answer right away, which is weird, but finally she says, "Sure."

I start walking toward the parking lot, but Abbie doesn't move.

"Something wrong?" I ask.

"No. I'm just waiting for Hannah. I'm giving her a ride, too."

"Oh. Okay." Something feels off. Abbie is standing there, watching the gym door, not talking, which is unusual. Abbie loves to talk. The silence is making me crazy. I tap, tap, tap Abbie on the shoulder. "So where is she?"

"Here she comes."

Hannah's running over to us. She's carrying her books in her hands, even though she has her backpack with her, which I think is strange. Before

I can ask, Abbie tells us to hurry. "I'm sure Mom is wondering where we are."

When we get in the car, Mrs. Anderson smiles at me. "Abbie didn't tell me you were sleeping over tonight, too."

Before I can react, Abbie says, "I told Izzy we'd bring her home. She missed the bus."

Mrs. Anderson bites her lip. "Oh. Okay. How's your mother doing, Izzy?"

"Fine, thank you."

The rest of the drive is done in total silence. I can't believe that Abbie invited Hannah for a sleepover and not me! I want to punch, punch, punch her. I want to punch Hannah, too. I fight back the tears and the grunt that are pushing to come out. I will not let any of them see how much I hurt.

After Mrs. Anderson drops me off, I watch the car disappear down the street. I'm glad Mom isn't home and that the house is empty. When I get inside I scream until my throat hurts. I throw my backpack across the room. It hits an end table and almost knocks down a lamp. I wish I had broken it.

I run up to my room and curl up on my bed and cry until there are no tears left. I knew Hannah would be trouble, but I didn't think she'd steal my best friend and that the two of them would push me out. Right now, I hate both of them.

When I finally settle down a little, I grab my phone and text Abbie.

I can't believe u did this to me. This isn't how best friends act. U hurt me. I will never forget this.

I read it over, press send and wait. A few minutes pass, then—

It's not what you think. Hannah's parents have to go away for a couple of days and she asked if she could stay with us. I didn't dis U.

If it was so innocent why didn't U just tell me?

Because you've been really pissy lately and I thought if I told U about Hannah, you'd get mad. And I was right.

You'd be mad if I did that to U!

No I wouldn't. I'd understand. Besides, there's no rule that U can't have more than one friend.

That's only true when you *have* more than one friend. But I'm not going to say that. I'm not going to say anything. Let her have her sleepover with Hannah. I don't care. I don't care one bit.

CHAPTER Twenty-One

I didn't sleep much last night. This has not been a good week. First the scrimmage and the double-play, then the sleepover. Make that the not-getting-invited-to sleepover. All I want to do is get this day over with and go home and sleep.

When I get to first period, I put my books down on my desk and make a point of ignoring Abbie, which is hard since she sits right next to me. I also ignore Billy Parker, who sits behind me and is a total pain. I'm, like, one of his favorite targets, but today I am not in the mood to be picked on.

Unfortunately, he has a major attitude this morning. One that involves bugging me. He grabs my pen, laughing as he waves it around.

I jump out of my seat and yell at him, "Stop being such a jerk, and give me back my pen!"

At first, he's surprised. I usually don't stand up for myself. But then his eyes light up.

"Make me," he says, holding my pink pen above his head, just beyond my reach. "What's so special about it anyway, *Dizzy*? It's just a dumb *pink* pen." Billy laughs his stupid laugh. "Who uses a *pink* pen?"

"You wouldn't understand, jerkhead." Grunting, I bend over, touch the floor. He laughs.

I'm not about to tell him it's the pen Dad gave me for my birthday last year. That it has black ink. Not blue. That ever since he gave it to me I can only write with black ink—even though sometimes I'd like to use blue. I just can't.

Billy tosses the pen to Mike who tosses it to Christopher who tosses it back to Billy. The whole class is watching. Even Jamie Barnes. Tears threaten to leak from my eyes. I hold them back. I will not cry in front of this silly, stupid boy.

"Billy likes Izzy," someone in the back of the class says. A couple of other kids pick it up, sing-songing, "Billy likes Izzy. Billy likes Izzy."

Billy snorts out a laugh. "Get real! Who could like someone who"—he does a perfect imitation of my grunt—"does that all the time?" He laughs again, and this time some of the other kids laugh, too.

My whole body starts to shake. I clench and unclench my hands, trying to control my anger, but I can't stop myself. I pull my hand back and swing, as hard as I can, and hit Billy Parker square in the stomach. He staggers back and is about to fall, but Christopher catches him. Maybe now Billy Parker will think twice before he picks on me.

Of course, that's when Mrs. Morgan comes into the room. "Sorry I'm late, but—" She stops in the middle of her announcement and looks our way. Billy is sitting in his seat, holding his stomach, rocking and moaning. I'm standing over him, my hands in fists. "What's going on?" Mrs. Morgan asks.

Amy Robins goes up to Mrs. Morgan, her face red with excitement. She's not called "Tattle Tale Amy" for nothing. "Billy stole Isabella's pen and wouldn't give it back, so Isabella got real mad and punched him in the *stomach*."

Mrs. Morgan shakes her head. "Thank you, Amy. You can go back to your seat now."

"I think I'm going to throw up." Billy mumbles and moans again, really loudly.

I look around the room. Everyone is staring at me, their eyes wide with shock. Slowly the rage leaves, and I realize what I've done. I've had a total meltdown. Once in a while, I get really angry at home where I feel safe enough to let go. But never in school. In school, I can usually hold it in.

Mrs. Morgan claps her hands and waits for everyone to quiet down. She nods toward Christopher, who is sitting behind Billy. "Go with Billy to the nurse's office," she says. "Make sure he's okay."

Next she points at me, crooks her finger.

While I'm walking up the aisle, she gives the class an assignment. All I can think about is what's going to happen next.

Everybody's eyes, including Jamie's, are glued on me as I walk to the front of the room. I keep my head up, face forward, and pretend not to notice. But I have my arms folded across my chest, my hands hidden so I can tap, tap, tap with my fingers without anybody seeing.

When I reach Mrs. Morgan's desk, she walks me out to the hall, and closes the classroom door. "Isabella." She sighs, shakes her head. "What were you thinking?"

I lower my head. What do I tell her? I don't know what got into me. I just know that at first it felt good, and then it didn't.

"I'm so sorry, Mrs. Morgan." My voice shakes and tears fill my eyes.

"I know you get teased a lot, Izzy. You usually handle it. What was different this time?"

I grunt, shrug my shoulders.

Mrs. Morgan bends down and looks into my eyes. "I'm sorry, but I have to send you to the principal's office. I know Billy provoked you, but there's no excuse for hurting another student."

I hang my head down so low my chin is almost touching my chest. "I know." Grunt. Touch the floor.

"I'll have Abbie walk you there. Wait here."

I wipe the tears away with the palms of my hands. Abbie! She's mad at me, too, after those texts I sent her. What am I going to say to her?

A minute later, she comes out. Shaking her head, she says, "I don't understand what's going on with you. You've been acting crazy lately. I can't believe you *hit* Billy. I mean, he's a jerk and all, but—"

"I don't know what's wrong with me. Everything's bothering me. I get so angry, and I can't stop myself."

Tears fill my eyes. I stick my hands in my jeans pocket, but instead of a tissue I find a little white pill. And it hits me. I haven't taken my meds for at least two weeks. Maybe longer. Could that be what's wrong?

I glance up at Abbie. I could lose my best friend because of those stupid pills. I'm not going to let that happen. "I'm sorry I was so mean to you and Hannah. You should be able to have other friends if you want." It hurts saying it, but I know it's true.

"Just because I like Hannah doesn't mean I don't like you."

"Yeah. I know." I wipe my eyes on my sleeve. "I think I know why I'm getting so angry, but I don't have time to explain it. Can we talk tonight?"

"Yeah, sure."

"About Hannah. Tell her I'm sorry for being such a jerk." I tap, tap, tap Abbie's shoulder.

"You can tell her when you see her. I'm sure she'll understand." She leans in and gives me a hug, which helps make things a little less awful. At least we're friends again.

"I guess we better get going." I touch the ground, stand and grunt. "My parents are going to kill me when they find out!"

As we walk down the hallway, I stop and tap, tap, tap softly on every door we pass. Abbie tries to get me to move on, but it's no use. I can't help myself.

CHAPTER TWENTY-TWO

"Suspended for a week!" Mom frowns, shakes her head. "I am so disappointed in you, Izzy. I don't know what to say."

We're sitting in her car in the school parking lot. The bell will ring soon, and kids will start coming out. I don't want them to see me. But I can't stand when she's mad at me, and I can't stop the words from tumbling out.

"I love you, Mom."

Mom closes her eyes, takes a breath. She knows what I need to hear. But first she needs a few seconds to calm herself.

"I love you, Mom!" I say again.

Finally she says the words. "I love you, too."

"Can we leave now?" I grunt and tap, tap, tap Mom's shoulder.

She starts the car, but before she pulls out, she turns to me. "Please tell me what got into you. I still can't believe you hurt that boy."

"He was a jerk, Mom. He took my pen and wouldn't give it back."

Mom rubs her temple and sighs.

"And he made fun of me. He imitated my grunt.

It sounded so stupid. *I sound stupid.*"

Mom's face softens. "I know how all this must hurt, Izzy. But Billy has done this to you before. You never lashed out like that."

I reach down and touch the carpet on the floorboard. When I sit back up, I stare out the side window.

"Well?" Mom asks. "What made this time so different?"

"I love you, Mom."

"Izzy—"

"Can you just please say it?"

She sighs. "I love you, too."

I grunt and touch the floor again. Finally, I get up the courage to tell her. "I forgot to take my medicine." I stare out the window. I don't want to see Mom's face when she hears this.

I wait for her to explode, but she doesn't say anything at first. After a minute, she says, "Look at me, Izzy."

I turn my head toward her.

"Is today the first day you missed?"

I bite my lip. "I love you, Mom."

Mom narrows her eyes. "How long has it been since you last took them?"

I start rocking in the seat. "I love you, Mom!"

Mom stops. Takes a breath. "I love you, too. Now how long?"

I shrug. "A few days maybe."

"How many days is 'a few'?"

I turn my face to the window again.

"Izzy!"

"Okay, so maybe I've skipped it for a week." It's more like two, but I can't bring myself to admit to that. She'll be mad enough about the one week.

"You what? Izzy, how many times have we told you—"

"I know. I know!" I grunt again. I still won't look at her. "I hate taking that stuff."

Mom puts her hand on my shoulder. "Izzy."

She waits.

Finally, I turn to face her.

She takes in a deep breath. Lets it out. "You can't just stop taking these drugs cold turkey." When she sees the confusion in my eyes, she explains, "You have to get off them gradually, Izzy. If you stop all at once you can get sick. Or worse. You could totally lose it, like you did today. You're lucky Billy didn't fall and break an arm or something. Do you understand what I'm saying?"

I nod. If I speak, I know I'll start to cry.

"I'm going to make an appointment with your doctor. See what she says." Mom looks at me with narrowed eyes. "Since you'll be home all week, we won't have to worry about pulling you out of school."

"I'm sorry." I whisper. "I love you, Mom."

Mom hands me a tissue to wipe the tears that have spilled down my cheeks. "I love you, too." She puts the car in gear, and we head out of the parking lot, neither of us talking.

When Dad gets home from work, Mom tells him about my suspension. Dad doesn't believe her at first. "You're kidding, right?"

"It's true." I croak, like the words are stuck in my throat and don't want to come out.

Dad pulls his hand through his hair, leaving it sticking up in places. "I don't understand. You would never hit or hurt anyone."

Mom doesn't say anything. Neither do I.

"Somebody talk to me!"

I grunt. Tap, tap, tap Dad's shoulder. He looks at me. "What happened, Izzy?"

I tell him about the pen and the teasing.

"That's it? That's what provoked you?"

I stay silent.

"Tell him the rest," Mom says.

Looking down, I mumble, "I didn't take my pills for the past week."

"What do you mean you didn't take them? What did you do with them?"

"I threw them away." Grunt. Touch the floor.

"You *what*?"

I bite my lip, keep my head down.

"Izzy, I asked you a question."

I lift my head. Dad is sitting at the table, his eyes narrowed and angry. "We don't give the meds to you lightly. We do our research and check with several doctors before we give you anything. We're trying to help you, and you just throw them away!"

"I hate them!" My stomach churns, and I feel like I might throw up.

"That's no excuse. You're responsible for your actions." When I don't say anything, Dad sits there, staring at me. Finally, in a calmer voice, he says, "You've left us little choice. You're grounded for two weeks. No overnights with Abbie. No Jump 'N Fun, beach, swimming—whatever."

I look at Mom for help. "Two whole weeks? The school only suspended me for one week."

"I agree with your father," Mom says.

"That's not fair!" I ball my hands into fists.

My anger is like a giant balloon, filling up with so much water another drop will make it burst. I feel the pressure building, building.

I want to kick the chair. Punch a wall. Instead, I scream at them. "You don't understand anything. You don't know what it's like to be me."

"Stop it, Izzy," Mom says.

But the balloon has burst. There's no putting it back together. "I hate you! I hate you both!" I see the pain in their faces, but right now I don't care. "You're the worst parents in the world."

Dad gets up and points toward the stairs. "Go to your room right now, young lady."

I stand there, fists still clenched, head up, not moving one inch.

"Now!" Dad slaps his hand on the table.

I grunt out a scream and sweep my books off the table with my hand.

"Izzy!" Mom cries out.

"I hate you!" I yell again. Sobbing, I run up the stairs, slam my door shut, and press my face into my pillow, screaming into it until I'm totally worn out.

CHAPTER TWENTY-Three

I must have fallen asleep, because the buzzing of my cell phone startles me awake. I glance at the screen. It's Abbie.

"How'd it go with your parents?" she asks.

"Not good." My head is pounding, and my throat is dry. "Hold on a second." I put down the phone and go to the bathroom. Splash some cold water on my face and drink some water.

The rage is gone. Now I'm just tired.

I go back to my room and pick up my phone. "I'm grounded for two whole weeks." I grunt. I so wish this tic would pass. It makes my throat feel sore all the time.

"Two weeks! Bummer."

I plop on the bed, put my arm over my eyes to keep the tears from spilling out.

"Izzy? Are you still there?"

"Yes," I croak. "Give me a sec."

I grab a tissue, blow my nose, and take a deep breath. I let it out slowly and after a grunt or two, I'm ready to talk. "Remember today when you asked why I was so angry all the time?"

"Yeah. You said you'd tell me about it later."

"Well, I'm pretty sure it's because I stopped taking my meds a week ago. Actually, it's more like two weeks, but my parents don't know that."

"Wow. Why? I mean, I know you don't like taking them, but that's pretty radical."

"I hated the way they made me feel. Plus, I was always hungry, and my clothes were getting tight, and I was tired all the time. And I wanted to have more energy for softball. So I decided to stop taking them."

"I wish you would have told me."

I shrug, even though I know she can't see me. "I didn't think it was that big a deal. I sure as heck didn't think I would lose it and get in trouble if I stopped." I sigh. "Anyway, my parents freaked out. They said it was dangerous to just quit like that. And, of course, they're mad about the Billy thing."

"Yeah, that was something to see." Abbie lowers her voice. "You didn't hear it, but when you and Mrs. Morgan were in the hall, everybody said Billy deserved it. Nobody likes him."

"Still, I shouldn't have punched him." I don't add that I am glad I did.

"Ummm ..." Abbie hesitates. "I hope you don't mind. Coach asked me why you weren't at practice today, and I told her about what happened with Billy."

I swallow hard. With all that happened today, I'd forgotten about softball. "That's okay. She would have found out anyway. I hope she won't kick me off the team."

"Maybe if you explain about the meds and all, she'll understand."

"Maybe. I hope so anyway."

"Well, at least you can go to the dance. Your grounding will be over by then, right?"

"I guess." I'm too tired to think about anything more right now. "I have to go. Mom is calling me down to dinner." Another lie.

I click off the connection before she can say anything. I thought I'd cried myself dry, but I was wrong. There seems to be plenty left.

An hour later, I head down the stairs. The scent of Mom's homemade spaghetti sauce fills the house. The table is set, and Mom is putting out the food when I get to the kitchen.

"I'm so sorry. I didn't mean any of that stuff I said." I try not to cry, but I can't stop the tears. "I love you, Mom."

Mom looks up at me. She tilts her head, sighs. "I love you, too." I run over to her and bury my face in her neck. "I know, sweetheart. It'll be okay."

Dad comes into the room. I turn to him. His face still has that pinched look on it. I don't know if it's because he's upset about the pills or angry with me for throwing a fit.

"I'm sorry, Dad." The words don't come out easily. They're stuffed down deep because of the tears. And the shame.

He sits in his chair. Blows out a breath. "Mom and I have been discussing this situation. We want to help make your life easier, Izzy, not harder. So Mom's made an appointment with your doctor. Maybe we can adjust the dosage or change the medication. Let's see what she has to say."

I tap, tap, tap Dad's shoulder. Lean over and hug him. "Thanks, Dad. I love you."

He smiles. "I love you, too. And you'll do

whatever the doctor suggests?"

"I promise," I say.

"Then let's put this all behind us."

"About softball—"

"It's a school activity. It's fine."

"Will you talk to Coach Grant about what happened?"

He nods. "Sure. I wanted to meet her anyway. Well, not under these circumstances, but sure. I'll talk to her."

Relieved, I take a shaky breath, wipe my eyes with my sleeve. "Thanks."

Dad nods.

One good thing has come out of this. I'll have that dress I bought for the dance paid for in chores in no time. I don't have anything else to do in the next two weeks.

CHAPTER Twenty-Four

Mom knocks on my door. "It's 7 a.m. Time to get up!"

I pull the covers over my head. It's my first full day of suspension, and I figured I would sleep late. Mom has other ideas.

"No sleeping in for you, young lady. We're keeping your school schedule. Up at seven, bed at 10."

Groaning, I stand and stretch. "Can I at least wear shorts and not school clothes?"

"Don't get fresh with me."

I'm not being fresh. I'm serious. But I let it drop and slip into my shorts and a tank top. After I make my bed and clean up the breakfast dishes, Mom gives me a choice—help her with the laundry or read a book. I love books, but it's 7:30 in the morning. I can't read all day. I try to get her to play basketball, but she says she has too much to do. So I help with the laundry.

I find out the hard way that you shouldn't put a red shirt in with white sheets. Now Mom has pink sheets for her bed. I'm not sure Dad's going to be happy with that color.

I have a feeling this is going to be a loooooooong week.

Abbie calls late that afternoon. It's so good to hear her voice. I can't wait to find out about school and practice. Anything that's not about chores!

"How's it going at home?" Abbie asks.

"I'm so bored! This staying home stuff sucks. How was practice?"

"The same as usual. I did see your dad, though. When I passed by Coach's office, he was in there with her."

I start pacing, "Could you hear what they were saying?"

"No. They were talking quietly. I couldn't get close enough."

"How did they look? Were they smiling? I hope my dad wasn't too intense. He can get that way sometimes, especially where I'm involved."

"It didn't look like anyone was upset. I didn't stay long. I didn't want them to see me and think I was snooping or anything."

I stop pacing, tap the phone on the bed three times, bend over to touch the floor, then sit at my desk. Abbie is used to the long pauses. "Thanks for trying."

"Sure. Sorry I couldn't be more helpful. I have to go. My mom's yelling for me to come down to help with dinner. I'll call you tomorrow when I get home."

"Okay. Thanks."

The rumble of the garage door opening vibrates my bedroom walls. Dad must have left work early to talk to Coach then come straight home. I grab my glove and run down the stairs.

"Abbie called and told me she saw you in Coach's office," I say as soon as he walks in the door. "What did she say?"

He sets his briefcase on the floor by the door. "Hello to you, too."

"Sorry, Dad. I'm just so nervous."

Dad sits on the couch, pats the pillow next to him. I touch the floor, punch, punch, punch my glove, and plop down beside him.

"She said that a suspension from school is serious stuff and often means suspension from the team as well."

"You mean she's throwing me off the team!" I can't breathe. She can't do this. I worked so hard.

"I didn't say that, Izzy. Let me finish."

He waits until I calm down, which takes some time while I tap and grunt and touch.

"We talked for quite a while. I told her about how you get teased a lot and that you usually don't let it get to you."

That's not true. It *always* gets to me. But I try not to react because that will only make things worse, especially with Billy. It's just that this time I couldn't hold it in.

"She understands some of what you have to deal with," Dad continues. "But she wants to talk to you before she decides what to do."

Wiping away the tears of frustration, I poke, poke, poke Dad in the shoulder. "Thanks for talking to her."

Dad sighs and gives me a hug. "How about I get changed, and we go swing the bat. The two of us can practice every day. Maybe Abbie and Hannah can come over sometimes, too. The four of us can practice plays. It'll be great."

"Why bother? I may not even be on the team."

"Coach didn't say she was kicking you off the team, Izzy. She said she wanted to talk to you before she made any decisions. You can show her how much you've improved while on suspension. That will help your cause."

"What about Mom. Do you think she'll be okay with me inviting Abbie and Hannah over to practice? Remember, I'm grounded for the next two weeks."

Dad hesitates, like he forgot about the grounding in his excitement over softball. "You're not leaving the house, right? You're just practicing softball. I'm sure Mom will understand."

Dad kisses my cheek and heads up the stairs, whistling the whole way. I hope he's right about Mom. After having me around all day, I think she might be happy to have me distracted by something besides me pestering her to play basketball.

I open the fridge to grab a bottle of water. Before I would grab a snack, too. But not now. Not since stopping my meds. My parents thought it would be safer to wait until we see the doctor before taking anything. I've managed to keep in the rage. Being home is a lot less stressful than being at school.

What a mess I've made of things. I hate, hate, hate that I have to start taking medicine again. But I hate worse that I lost control. That I hurt someone, even though it was stupid Billy. What if I'd gotten so angry that I hurt Hannah? Or Abbie! Maybe there's a way—

"I see Dad's home."

I jump at the sound of Mom's voice. "I didn't hear you come in."

"You were lost in thought. Want to share?"

I shake my head. "It's nothing."

I have an idea but I'm not ready to share it yet. I'm going to have to do some research, but I have a lot of free time on my hands. Maybe there is another way to get help. Maybe without having to take meds.

CHAPTER Twenty-Five

Mom is fine with Abbie and Hannah coming over for practice. She's really getting into softball, especially after coming to the scrimmage and seeing how important it is to me. But tonight it's just Dad and me. I quit early, telling Dad I have some stuff I want to do. I don't tell him that stuff is research on other ways to deal with tics and obsessions. I want to find out as much as I can before I say anything to my parents.

I type "*natural ways to treat Tourette Syndrome*" in the search engine. A ton of sites and suggestions come up. Things like behavioral and counseling therapies, EEG biofeedback, homeopathy, bodywork, energy medicine, herbal medicine, Chinese medicine. I have no idea what any of this stuff means.

When I look them up, I'm more confused than ever. Then I find a book that says it's a guide for natural treatments. If I can get my parents to buy it, maybe they'll find some other way to treat my TS, and I won't have to take the meds.

I copy down the name, head downstairs to where my parents are watching TV. When I walk into the room, Dad hits the pause button.

"Hey, Izzy. What's up?" he asks.

"I have something I want to show you."

Mom pats the seat beside her. "Come sit."

I tap, tap, tap the seat and sit on the edge so I can see both of them.

"I've been doing some research on Tourette's." I almost laugh when I see both of their faces, eyebrows up, eyes wide. "Why do you both look so surprised?"

Mom answers. "It's a good surprise, sweetheart. It's just that you never showed much interest before in learning about TS."

"Yeah, well, I was too busy dealing with it. Besides I was young and that was before—you know. Anyway, I was looking for something else that we could do. Something that didn't have me taking medicine." Again that surprised look. "There was a whole bunch of stuff that I didn't understand. Then I found this book"—I hand the paper with the name of the book to Mom—"and I thought that maybe you could buy it, and we could see if there's anything in there that might help me."

I sit on my hands to keep from tapping Mom, but I can't stop my feet from bouncing while I wait for their answer.

"Wow," Dad says. "Good for you, Izzy. I like that you're being proactive." He turns to my mom. "What do you think, Jen?"

Mom nods her head. "It's certainly worth looking into. I'll order it and have them ship it right away. Maybe it will come before your doctor's appointment on Thursday."

"Do we *have* to go? Couldn't we try something

different first?"

"Yes," Mom says, "we have to go. Dad and I are more than willing to look into an alternative to drugs for you, Izzy. But I also want to talk to your doctor about it. And, considering what happened at school, I don't think we should wait while we explore other methods of help."

I take a deep breath and blow it out. At least they're willing to look into it. I guess it's a start.

"Okay." Now I let myself tap, tap, tap Mom's shoulder. "Thanks."

Before I leave the room, I turn to my parents. "I love you, Mom. I love you, Dad."

Dad smiles. He even beats Mom to the "I love you, too" response.

CHAPTER Twenty-Six

I thought going back to school after being suspended would be totally embarrassing, but nobody makes fun of me. In fact, some of the kids act like getting suspended is cool.

Except for Billy. He must have saved up spitballs while I was home, because he keeps hitting me with them all through math class. I ignore him. I am not about to start something and get suspended again.

The school day finally ends, and it's time to face Coach.

I'm so nervous my stomach hurts. My tics are so bad it takes me forever at my locker, and my touch-the-ground tic, which I do three or four times on my way to the field, slows me down even more. I'm totally late getting to practice. Warm-up is over and everyone is in position, tossing balls around.

Coach is standing alone on the sideline, watching. I walk up behind her, clench my fists, try not to poke her shoulder with my finger. But I can't stop myself.

Poke. Poke. Poke.

She jumps and turns around. When she sees it's me, she lifts her eyebrows. "Nice of you to show up," she says.

"Sorry, Coach. I know you wanted to talk to me but—" I don't want to tell her I was so nervous my tics made me late. I don't want to use them as an excuse all the time.

She nods toward the dugout. "We'll have our conversation in there."

I try to say okay but it comes out in a grunt.

"Abbie," Coach calls out. "Hit some practice balls to the team. I'll be back in five."

I follow Coach to the dugout. She sits on the bench and waits for me to take a seat beside her.

"So." She stops and looks at me. Her eyes are all squinty. I can't tell if she's mad or confused. I punch, punch, punch my glove and follow that tic with a grunt. "Your dad told me what happened between you and this other student," Coach finally says. "His name is Billy, right?"

If I try to talk I'll grunt, so I nod instead.

"I checked with some of the teachers. They say he's a bully. I imagine this wasn't the first time he picked on you."

I shrug.

"I'll take that as a yes. I was also told you've never gotten physical before. Why did it bother you so much this time?"

"Didn't my dad tell you?"

"I want to hear it from you."

I swallow. I hate talking about it, but I have to tell her the truth. If I don't, she'll find out and never trust me again. That thought makes my stomach hurt even more.

"I stopped taking my medicine. Mom said I shouldn't have stopped all of a sudden like that. It made me moody, and I got mad a lot."

"Why did you stop taking it?"

I bend over, touch the ground. Sit up, tap Coach on her shoulder. Then I start punching my fist into my glove. Coach watches me, waiting me out.

I swallow, take a breath. This is even harder than I thought it would be. "Actually, I pretended to take the pills, then threw them in the garbage."

She lifts her eyebrows, tilts her head.

"I was hoping I'd be okay without them," I say. "I don't like the way they make me feel." Grunt. Touch the ground. "While I was on suspension Mom took me to the doctor, and she adjusted the dose on one and took me off the other. Plus, she's going to test me for allergies. She says that might be one of the reasons for my tics and stuff. And we talked about trying other ways to help that don't include drugs."

"Okay," Coach says. "Sounds like you and your parents are trying hard to make your life a little easier."

I start talking fast, filling in the silence. I don't want her to think that she can't trust me after all that's happened. "I learned my lesson. Honest. I promise I'll do everything the doctor and my parents say. Please don't kick me off the team."

"Is that what you think is going on here, Izzy?"

"I don't know. Dad said that's what happens sometimes with kids who get suspended."

She pauses for a minute, which feels more like an hour. "You know, when your dad talked to me, he was adamant about how you hardly ever get mad, even though over the years you've gotten teased and bullied a lot of the time. If that happened to me, I might lose my temper once in a while, even if I did take medicine for it. Not that I'm saying what you did was right. Just that I understand where you were coming from."

Am I hearing her right? Tears sting my eyes. She gets what I'm going through. I squeeze my arms and legs tight to my body so I won't tic. I even hold my breath so I won't grunt. I want to hear every word she says.

"I'm not throwing you off the team, Izzy, but I'm going to bench you for four games. Your actions have to have some consequences, but I'm also aware that there were extenuating circumstances."

"So I'm still on the team, but I can't play right away." I feel good and bad at the same time.

"That about sums it up," Coach says. "Now go to your right field position. *And* keep your focus."

"But I thought you said I couldn't play for four games."

"I said you couldn't play in *games*. I didn't say you couldn't practice."

I'm feeling better with each word Coach says. I draw in a deep breath and let it out real slow, until I feel like I can stand without ticking. "Thank you, Coach." I start to leave, then turn. "I promise I will never get mad at anybody again."

"That's a tough promise for anyone to keep, Izzy. Just make sure your head's in the game and give a 100 percent and you'll do fine. Now get out there. You've missed enough practices."

It's better than I'd hoped for. I want to prove

to Coach, and to myself, that I can do this, just like the other normal girls on the team. Plus, I have time to practice and improve before I go on the field to play a real game again. Maybe by then I'll be over that double play. Maybe by then I'll even be able to *assist* on a double play against another team.

I run out of the dugout and onto the field. As I pass Abbie and Hannah, they each give me a high five. Joy fills up my belly and when, along the way, I get the touch-the-ground tic, I turn it into a cartwheel.

I may not be back on the team yet, but I'm on my way.

CHAPTER Twenty-Seven

I saw a video on Facebook a while ago of a horse that opened the gate of his stall with his teeth and took off at a run, happy to be free. That's how I feel today. Out of my stall. Free.

It's Friday afternoon, and I'm going to my first overnight after two very long weeks of being grounded. I'm staying at Abbie's house tonight, but first her parents are taking us out to dinner. Hannah will be there, too. The thing is the more time I spend with Hannah the more I like her. I'm glad she's sleeping over, too.

"Izzy," Mom calls up to me from the bottom of the stairs. "The Andersons will be here any minute. Are you ready?"

"I'll be right down," I say. I check my backpack. Top and shorts to sleep in. Swim suit and towel for the beach tomorrow. My toothbrush, hairbrush, make-up. What am I missing? I glance around my room. I've packed everything I'd set out.

"Izzy!" Mom calls again.

"I'm coming!" Whatever it is I'm forgetting, Abbie can loan to me.

Mom is waiting for me at the bottom of the

steps. She's holding a plastic bag in her hand, wiggling it back and forth for me to notice. "Your pill for tomorrow morning. Until the doctor says—"

"I know." That's what I was forgetting. "I was on my way to the kitchen to get it." Which was almost true. I would have if I'd remembered.

"Uh huh. You won't forget to take it tomorrow, right? I don't have to call and remind you, do I?"

"No, Mom. I promise I'll take the pill. I'll ask Abbie to remind me. She never forgets anything."

Mom hands me the baggie, pushes my hair behind my ears. "I found a homeopathic doctor. He's in Tampa. I made an appointment for you. It's in three weeks."

I stuff the baggie in my backpack. "Homeo what?"

"I read that book you found, and the author suggested homeopathy as an alternative to drugs. It's a natural approach, like you asked for. I thought we'd give it a try."

I give Mom a kiss on the cheek. "Thanks." I lean in and give her a hug. "I love you, Mom."

"I love you, too. In the meantime—"

"I know. I'll take the meds." I rush out the door before she pins a reminder note on me. Okay. I'm exaggerating. But only a little.

Later, I look around the big room where Abbie's parents have taken us for dinner. "This is so cool." I say. "I've never been to a Japanese Steakhouse before. Thanks, Mr. and Mrs. Anderson."

We're sitting around a large, half-moon shaped table with a big, shiny griddle in the middle of it. Another table just like it is across from us. Standing between them is our chef, cooking our meal. Right there in front of us.

I took the seat at the end of the table so if I get the urge—like I have right now—to tap somebody's shoulder, it will be Abbie that I poke and not Mr. or Mrs. Anderson.

A few minutes, later three people walk in: two adults and a little girl in a wheelchair with three silver balloons attached to it. One has "Happy Birthday" written on it. Another has the number 9, and the third says, "Let's Party!" The hostess sits them at the table directly across from us.

The dad attaches a special booster seat to the restaurant chair and checks to make sure it doesn't wiggle. Then the mom lifts the birthday girl onto it and straps her in. The little girl sees me watching. She smiles and tries to wave, but her hands and arms don't move very well. I smile and wave back to her.

Abbie grabs my arm. "Oh. My. God."

"What?" I follow the direction of her eyes.

Coming in late and getting into the seat at the end of the table, right there across from us, is Jamie Barnes.

CHAPTER TWENTY-EIGHT

Jamie is sitting next to his dad, checking out the menu. I'm about to call to him to say hi when he looks up and sees me staring at him. His face turns a deep red. Before I can even wave, he looks down at the menu again. If he'd just nodded, I might have been able to let it go. But now, I can't stop watching him.

When he sees that I'm still staring, he gets up and walks over to his mom. Whispers in her ear. She puts her hand on his forehead. Frowns.

"What's wrong?" Jamie's dad asks.

His mom answers, but her voice is too low for me to hear what she says.

Mr. Barnes folds his arms across his chest. "Why didn't you say something before we left?" Jamie shrugs, and Mr. Barnes sighs loudly enough for all of us to hear. "Do I have to drive you home?"

Jamie shakes his head. "Give me the keys. I'll go lie down in the car."

His mom gets up and gives him a hug. She says something else I don't hear. She must be worried, because Jamie says, "I'll be okay. Don't rush. Let Katie enjoy herself."

He glances at us, looks away and rushes toward the exit. I try not to turn around and watch him as he leaves. I know how it feels to have people stare. It happens all the time when I tic. But I can't stop myself. When he reaches the exit, he glances back. I know because I'm still staring.

Abbie's voice pulls my attention back to the table. "What do you think got into him?"

I look back, but Jamie is gone.

"Looks like he got sick or something," I say.

The chef starts serving the food, right off the grill. We stop talking about Jamie. I watch his sister while I eat. Her mother feeds her from jars filled with stuff that looks like baby food. She smiles a lot, especially when her mother leans over and whispers in her ear. Her dad keeps checking the chair to make sure it's attached right. He fusses over her a lot, too.

Just as we're leaving, they bring out a birthday cake with nine candles on it. It's hard to believe that the tiny little girl sitting in the chair is that old. She looks more like five or six.

When we get outside, Jamie is sitting on the curb, fiddling with his phone. I guess he's waiting for his family to come out. When he sees us, I wave. He turns his head, gets up, and walks over to a car. He climbs into the back seat and lies down.

That's when I realize it. Jamie isn't sick. He's embarrassed. Embarrassed about being seen with his sister. And boy, does that make me mad.

CHAPTER Twenty-Nine

The weekend with Abbie and Hannah is fun, though every once in a while I think of Jamie and his sister. Okay, more than once in a while. Truth is I can't get it out of my mind. But I don't bring it up. It's not right to say something about someone when all you have is a hunch. A thought. No proof.

But Monday at lunch, when Hannah mentions how much fun the weekend was, especially the dinner at the restaurant, it pops out of my mouth like a hiccup or a sneeze.

"I think Jamie was embarrassed about his sister." Grunt. Tap, tap, tap.

Abbie and Hannah stare at me, like they don't know what I'm talking about.

"At the restaurant. Friday night. When he left as soon as he saw us." Another grunt.

"Where did that come from?" Abbie asks.

"I don't know. It's just been bothering me all weekend."

"What's to be embarrassed about?" Hannah asks. "She can't help it that she has problems."

"I know that, but why else would he act so strange?"

Abbie shrugs. "Maybe he really was sick."

"Then why was he sitting on the curb playing with his phone instead of lying down in the car like he said he would?"

Hannah clears her throat. "Ummm. I notice you mention Jamie a lot. Do you, like, have a crush on him?"

I tap, tap, tap the table. Bite my lip to keep the grunt down. I can feel the heat climbing up my neck and onto my face.

Abbie's eyes widen. "Oh my God, Izzy. Hannah's right. You do talk a lot about him. Are you crushing on him?"

Grunting, I say, "Can we talk about something else?"

I grab Abbie's apple. Throw it in the air. Catch it. Throw it again. This time I miss it, and it falls to the floor. I pick it up and hand it to Abbie.

Abbie looks at her now bruised apple, shakes her head. "Sure we can talk about something else. How about you trade me that apple for your bag of chips?"

We all laugh.

"I guess that's fair," I say.

Abbie grabs the bag before I can toss it and crush it in the catching act. I take a bite of the apple. It's juicy and sweet. I think I got the better end of that deal.

Hannah asks about Saturday's dance, and I tune out. What does Jamie have to be embarrassed about? Abbie never seems to be ashamed to be seen with me. And believe me, some of the stuff my body does—stuff I have no control over, like the poking or the obsessing—can be pretty embarrassing, especially when I do it in public, which is most of the time. I mean *I'm* embarrassed by me. But Abbie acts as if what I do is normal.

Maybe I was wrong getting mad at Jamie. Maybe it's something else that's bothering him.

The next day Jamie comes in just before Mrs. Morgan closes the door. All during class I stare hard at him, trying to get his attention, but he doesn't look at me once. When class ends, he's up and out of the room before the bell stops ringing. It's like he's trying to avoid me or something.

At first I think it's because of me seeing him steal those posters. Or maybe he noticed that I kind of like him and that freaks him out. But the more I think about it, I realize that Jamie always acted a little weird around me. He's never really mean. He just kind of avoids me.

Maybe he thinks Tourette Syndrome is something you can catch. Now that's just plain silly. Maybe I'll find a time where he can't run away and just ask him what his problem is. Maybe I'll do that real soon. Like Saturday. At the dance. Maybe I just will.

CHAPTER Thirty

"Come on, Izzy. It's just a stupid dance. Okay. It's a special dance just for the eighth graders, but you don't have to freak out over it."

Mom peeks around the bathroom door. "What are you mumbling about?"

I grunt and point the mascara wand at my face. "Look at me!" There's a big, black blotch on the upper corner of my right eye and another on the eyebrow of my left eye. "I've been trying for 20 minutes but I keep messing up." I tap, tap, tap the mascara wand on the edge of the sink in frustration. Now there's black goop there, too.

Mom comes over to me and gently takes the wand from my hand. "Maybe I can help with that."

I grunt and stamp my foot, upset at everything and everybody. Mom waits for me to settle down.

After a couple of minutes of grunting and stamping, I blow out a sigh. "Sorry. I love you, Mom."

"I love you, too."

I grunt again, flip the light switch on and off, then poke, poke, poke Mom on the shoulder. "I love you, Mom."

"I love you, too. You're really nervous about this dance, huh?"

I nod. Grunt. Poke.

Again, she waits. When my breathing steadies and I'm able to stop fidgeting, she asks, "Ready?"

"Yeah. I guess." I hold on to the bathroom sink to keep myself still.

Mom looks at me, finger to her lips, then smiles. "Easy peasy."

She dampens a tissue, cleans up where I missed and painted my face. Then she finishes putting the mascara on my lashes.

"Next," she says.

I hand her some lipstick. She looks at the deep brown color, shakes her head, and picks up a soft red. "This," she says, "is the perfect color for your skin tone, and it matches your new dress. That other stuff makes you look like a zombie."

I lift my hands, hold them like claws, and growl. Mom shakes her head and laughs. "Stand still, missy, or you'll look more like a clown."

When she's done she stands back, tilts her head, and smiles. "You are so beautiful, Izzy."

I turn and stare into the mirror. I'd put big rollers in my hair when it was wet and now it's falling in soft, brown waves around my face. And the mascara and lipstick—they make me look a lot older. That's when I realize I look a lot like my mom, and she's really pretty. If a guy—okay, I'm just going to say it—if Jamie can look past the weirdness, just maybe he'll think I'm pretty, too.

CHAPTER Thirty-One

The music is blasting when I walk into the school gym. Abbie and Hannah are already there. I join them, and we stand around swaying to the music, trying to talk over the noise. One by one, the rest of the team joins us.

"Hey." Meghan waves and slips between Abbie and me. She looks me up and down. Nods. "You look good in red, Izzy."

I'm surprised she's talking to me. She gets so annoyed at me when I mess up on the field. "Thanks." I gently tap, tap, tap her on the shoulder. "You look good in black."

Meghan shakes her head. "You are so strange sometimes." She looks Abbie over, glances down at her gold, strappy high-heeled shoes. "Those are pretty awesome! I want a pair."

"Thanks. I bought them with my babysitting money. Mom said they were too high and that I'd be sorry I wore them." Abbie scrunches up her nose. "I'll never admit it to her, but she's right. They hurt like crazy."

I glance down at my shoes. Actually, they're my mom's. We finally wear the same size and, though they're not real high, I think they're kind of cool. I bend down to touch them, and hide the tic by fooling around with the buckle.

When I look up, Mike from our English class is walking toward us. I clench my fists so I won't go poking at him. He asks Abbie to dance. After they leave, I relax.

Abbie is part way to the dance floor when she stops and calls out, "Wait!" A minute later, her shoes are off her feet and stashed under the snack table that holds the punch and chips. "Don't tell my mom," she says as she passes me. "I hate it when she's right."

Laughing, I give her a thumbs up.

Abbie comes back from her dance, and we stand around talking. After a few minutes, I notice Mike staring at Abbie from across the dance floor. His friends are punching him on the arm, laughing. Mike's face turns a bright red.

"Mike keeps looking at you," I say. "I think he likes you."

A smile spreads across her face. "Really? He is cute, isn't he?"

Before I can answer, Mike is heading our way again. I glance at Abbie. Her face is bright with excitement.

Abbie and Mike stay on the dance floor for the next few dances. Hannah is dancing with Tyler from history class. After a while, a couple of guys ask me to dance, too. I am having fun, sort of, but most of the time I'm looking for Jamie. When I finally see him, he's hanging out with a bunch of guys on the other side of the room.

The DJ is just coming back from his break.

Before I lose my nerve, I walk over to Jamie, straight across the empty dance floor. I don't know what exactly I'm going to say to him. Should I start with the posters? The bruises? Or maybe the dinner and Katie?

Jamie spots me coming just as the music starts up again. His face turns a bright red. He looks down at his feet, then up again at me. I stop walking. Maybe I should wait to talk to him. I mean it's so loud now with the music and all. Not knowing what to do, I lift my hand and wave.

He lifts his hand to wave back and—I can't believe this—Marci, the biggest flirt in the whole wide world, grabs it! She pulls him onto the dance floor, laughing and chattering away. Jamie follows. I mean what else could he do? She really is pushy.

The dance floor is starting to fill up with kids and I'm stuck there, in the middle, all alone, looking stupid. I detour around everybody, making my way to the snack table. From that safe distance, I watch as Marci and Jamie move across the floor. He's a really good dancer. I hadn't known that. So is Marci. Tears of frustration and anger blur my vision.

A loud grunt of frustration escapes me. I stand there alone, watching them, until the song ends. I'm not sure what to do next. Marci is gabbing away, not letting Jamie alone. I grunt and tap, tap, tap the snack table.

Out of the corner of my eye, I see somebody coming toward me. It's Abbie. She grabs my hand and pulls me toward the dance floor. "Come on," she says. "The team is dancing together for this one."

"I don't know." I try not to follow, but Abbie keeps tugging at me. "I'm not good at this group dancing stuff."

"Just follow me. It's easy."

We join the crowd sliding across the floor. I don't want to spoil Abbie's mood so I concentrate on the dance. After a few tries, I get the moves. Once I do, I love it. The music and the movement help me relax and forget about Jamie—almost.

Just about everyone is dancing, except Jamie. At least, I can't find him. I wonder if Marci is still latched onto him. I can't find her either.

As I dance, I add an occasional punch in the air, but no one seems to notice. We all beg the DJ to play one more line-dance, then another. After the third request, he says it's time for the last dance of the night. Slow and easy.

Mike asks Abbie to dance. Hannah and I make our way back to the snack table. Marci is dancing with Tyler, and Jamie is nowhere in sight. After the music stops, Mike walks Abbie over to us. I can tell by the blush on her face that she's had a great time.

"Yep," I say after he leaves. "Mike definitely likes you."

Abbie's grin widens. "I think I like him, too." Abbie reaches under the table for her shoes, which, fortunately, are still there where she stashed them earlier.

"Oooow!" she says as she struggles to pull them on. "Boy, they hurt!"

"Then don't wear them," I say.

"My mom's picking us up, remember? If she sees me carrying them she'll know she was right."

"So what's the big deal? They're only shoes."

"Because," Abbie grimaces as she walks, "the next time I want to buy cool shoes she'll remind me of tonight and say no."

"Oh, I get it," I say. But I really don't. Who wants to wear shoes that hurt?

Abbie walks between Hannah and me, holding onto our arms for support. When we get close to the car, she lets go.

"How was the dance?" Mrs. Anderson asks once we're settled in.

"Fun," Abbie says.

"And the shoes were okay?"

"Yep."

I almost blurt out about how Abbie ditched her shoes. I turn it into a grunt. Abbie looks at me, shakes her head.

I put my hand over my mouth, my eyes opened wide. I feel bad about kind of lying to Mrs. Anderson. Mom calls it lying by omission. But Abbie is my best friend, and best friends stick together.

Abbie pulls out her phone and texts Hannah and me.

Don't either of u make a big deal over this. I wasn't really lying. My shoes WERE okay. They were safely stashed under the snack table all night.

Before I can text back, Mrs. Anderson tells Abbie to put her phone away. "It's rude to text while your friends are sitting here in the car with you."

I bite my lip to stop from laughing.

"Sorry, Mom," she says but she finishes a text she'd started and hits send.

Her text comes a second later.

So do u think Mike really likes me?

Both Hannah and I give her a thumbs up, but we can't really say anything since Abbie's not supposed to be texting and she didn't ask the question out loud.

Mrs. Anderson shakes her head. "You can talk to each other with your voices and mouths, you know."

None of us say anything.

Mrs. Anderson sighs. "I swear. Cell phones have destroyed conversation."

If she only knew.

When I get home, Mom greets me at the door. She lifts my chin with her fingers and stares into my eyes. "Did you have a good time?"

I think about all that happened before I answer. I didn't get a chance to talk to Jamie, but I had a great time with my friends. Abbie was funny with her whole shoe thing, and I am happy for her and her maybe-new boyfriend. And the last couple of dances were a blast.

Easy decision.

"Yeah," I say. I tap, tap, tap her on the arm, lean over, and hug her tight. "It was a good night."

And in a lot of ways it was. But I still have to talk to Jamie!

CHAPTER Thirty-Two

Softball practice is almost over, and Jamie and the track team still haven't passed by the field. I keep looking, but—

"Palmer. Heads up." A high fly is coming my way. I turn and run, looking up, keeping my eyes on the ball. When it starts to drop, I reach out, and the ball lands just short of the glove's sweet spot. Dad's words echo in my head, "Cover the ball with your right hand so it doesn't fall out." So that's what I do.

I wave the ball in the air to show that I caught it. I can't stop a big smile from spreading across my face.

"Not bad, Palmer," Coach says. "But it would be a lot easier if you keep your head in the practice."

"Sorry, Coach." I punch, punch, punch my glove and stop myself just in time from doing a cartwheel.

A minute later, the track team comes running by. I watch Jamie, tagging along, last as usual.

"Palmer!" Coach shouts as the grounder she hit my way bounces by me. Darn! I. Will. Focus.

And I do for the rest of practice, which is all of

five more minutes. I'm walking toward Mom's car when I spot Jamie. He's walking toward a minivan parked in the lot. His little sister—Katie, that's what he called her at dinner—is strapped into a special seat in the back. She's looking out the window, trying to wave her hand.

Maybe I'm crazy, but it seems like she's looking at me. Does she remember me from the other night? I don't want to be rude so I wave back. Her lips turn up into a huge smile.

Jamie gets in the front seat, turns and says something to his sister. She looks at him and nods. As the car pulls away, Katie looks my way and waves again. Jamie follows her gaze. When he sees me staring back, he quick turns away. The car pulls out, and I'm more confused than ever.

Chapter Thirty-Three

At lunch, I find a note Mom put in my lunch bag. It says, "I love you, too!" I crumple it and put it in my jeans pocket. That particular tic has been bugging me for weeks. I can't hold a conversation with her—especially when I'm upset—without "I love you, Mom," pouring out of my mouth every other sentence. I think this is her way of saying she really doesn't mind, though it's driving me crazy. At least it's just Mom I say it to.

Oh my god! What if I said it to everyone?

I love you, Abbie.

I love you, Hannah.

I love you, Mrs. Morgan.

I love you, Jamie!

I look at Abbie, the words forming on my lips. I clamp my hand over my mouth. I will not say it.

Abbie tilts her head, her eyebrows pulled together. "What?"

I swallow the four words and shake my head. If I talk, I know they'll pop out. I grab my sandwich and take a bite. Now I don't have to talk.

Abbie nods. She gets that I'm going through something. "So," she says, "my parents agreed to the roller skating party. I can invite 17 kids. That's 20 with you, Hannah, and me."

That's right! Abbie will be 13 in a couple of weeks. She's two months and three days older than me, which makes me just a little jealous. Mom says in 20 years I'll be glad that I'm younger, but right now—

"Izzy. Did you hear me? I need your help with the invitation list."

I try to apologize for being distracted, but it comes out as a grunt. I grunt again in frustration. It's been a couple of weeks since I started taking the lower dose of that one pill. It's helped me with my anger issues, but the tics and distractions are as bad as ever. I can't wait to see the homeo-whatever doctor Mom was talking about. I have an appointment next week. Maybe he can help.

I swallow, take a deep breath, and blow it out slowly. "Sure, I'll help," I finally manage to get out.

Abbie acts as if nothing weird just happened. "Great. I've already made a list of girls to invite. I know we pretty much agree on them. It's the guys I need help with." She turns to Hannah. "I don't mean to leave you out of this conversation. If there's someone you want to invite, just tell me."

Hannah laughs. "Thanks, Abbie. I'm happy just to be going. You two make the list. I have to go to the girls' room."

Hannah leaves. Abbie doodles a heart on the paper with the list of names then scratches it out. "Now for the boys. Who should we start with?"

"How about Mike? I think he has a crush on you."

Abbie shakes her head. "I don't know. It has

been days since the dance and he hasn't even talked to me."

"I see how he stares at you in English. And he came to our practice the other day. I wouldn't be surprised if he asks me to ask you if you like him."

"He really is cute. And nice." Her face turns red. "Okay, Mike is on the list. Do you want me to ask Jamie? I can't tell how you really feel about him."

I grunt. Tap, tap, tap her arm. "Neither can I. It's not a crush. Well, maybe it is, but it's more than that. I've kind of liked him for a while, but when I saw him steal those posters—it got stuck in my head. I know that sounds silly, but—"

"No. I get it," Abbie says. "I've known you a long time, Izzy. You don't have to explain."

I bend, touch the ground, sit up, and sigh. "I want to explain. It's not just the posters. I might have gotten over that. But a few days later he came to school with a bad bruise on his side. A week or so later, he had a black eye. Then he acted so weird at the restaurant. They're all questions jumbled up in my mind and they keep replaying and replaying, like a song I can't get out of my head. I have to get to the bottom of it all or it will drive me crazy."

"Is it a part of your—what is it called again?"

"Obsessive-Compulsive Disorder. It started out that way. But when you put it all together, it's more. It's like a mystery. And"—heat tickles my cheeks—"he really is cute."

I scrunch down in my seat and hear the crackle of Mom's note in my pocket. I clamp my teeth together so I won't say, "I love you", and pull out the note and stick it in my lunch bag with my crumpled napkin and empty sandwich bag. Maybe if I throw it away I'll throw away the thought, too.

"If he comes to the party, I can talk to him there. Maybe then I can let it all go."

"Okay, I'll invite him to the party," Abbie says. "Now who else?"

We spend the rest of lunch figuring out the list of boys and other details of the party. Hannah helps us decide what music we want the DJ to play. My mind keeps going back to Jamie. Now that I've got a good chance of talking to him I'm wondering if I'll have enough nerve to actually do it.

CHAPTER Thirty-Four

It's the middle of a blazing hot, sunny day in late February, but inside the Stardust Skate Center it's like a cool, starry night. One with disco lights flashing and music blaring.

"Some of the girls said having a roller skating party was for babies," Abbie says.

It's Abbie's birthday. She should have whatever kind of party makes her happy. Why do people have to be so mean?

"Who said that?" I ask.

Abbie points to Meghan and Ashley. The two of them are skating with Dan, the tall, cute, and very popular center for the basketball team. They're on either side of him, holding onto his arms, laughing.

Meghan leans into Dan, grabbing his shoulder with her free hand like she's going to fall. Dan lets go of Ashley and grabs Meghan around the waist, steadying her. Ashley glares at Meghan, her face pinched with anger. Next thing you know, she's on the floor, her legs splayed out in front of her. I'm not sure if she fell on purpose or not, but Dan is right there helping her up.

"I guess they're right 'cause they're sure acting

like babies," I say.

Abbie bursts out laughing. "You are so right!"

I look around. The party started about 30 minutes ago and Jamie hasn't showed up yet. I don't know if I'm glad or not. I've been rehearsing what I'll say to him. It comes out different every time. And it always sounds stupid, no matter how I say it.

"He'll come. Don't worry," Abbie says. "He said he would."

The music stops and the DJ announces that he's going to play a game called Red Light, Green Light.

"Do you know what that is?" I ask Abbie.

"It's like Simon Says. When he says 'Green Light Go', you can skate. If he just says 'Go' and you move, you have to start back at the beginning."

"That I can do." I grab Abbie's hand and pull her onto the floor where we join up with Hannah.

In the middle of the game, I spot Jamie standing behind the half wall looking up at the disco ball. Since I'm watching Jamie and not where I'm going, I skate right into Abbie. She starts waving her arms, trying to get her balance. I try to help, but instead I end up pushing her into Meghan. The three of us fall down in a heap. The other skaters go around us while we untangle ourselves. Finally the DJ calls, "Red Light Stop."

I help Meghan up and tap, tap, tap her on the shoulder. "I'm so sorry," I say. "I got distracted and—"

She pushes my hand away. "You always get distracted, Izzy. Even on the ball field."

Abbie hooks her arm through mine and grabs

Meghan's hand. "Hey you two, the DJ just said, 'Green Light Go'. Come on. I want to win."

Meghan drops Abbie's hand. "I'm going to skate with Ashley. She hardly ever falls."

"Except when Dan's around," I say to her disappearing back.

Abbie laughs so hard I'm afraid she might fall without any help from me. Hannah, who's been hovering around waiting for us, asks, "What's so funny?"

"You had to be there," Abbie says.

I bite back a grunt, bend over, touch the ground. Stand and tap, tap, tap Abbie on the shoulder. "I think I'll sit the rest of this game out."

Abbie tilts her head. "Hey, it was no big deal. Everyone falls down once in a while."

"It's not that. Meghan doesn't bother me. She might be a great ballplayer, but she's such a drama queen. I'm not into her drama."

"Then why?"

"I think I saw Jamie. That's why I got distracted."

The game ends, and the DJ announces the start of another one.

"You two skate this one," I say. "I expect you to win."

"Okay. We'll catch up with you later when we have pizza and cake." Abbie and Hannah start to skate away. Abbie stops and turns toward me. "Good luck with your talk."

I give her a thumbs up, like I know it will go well. Truth is I'm scared. I still don't know how to say what I need to say to Jamie. Will he think I'm weird? Will he get mad?

Sighing, I start skating toward the closest exit.

That's where I see Jamie. Standing behind the wall.

And he's not looking at the disco ball anymore. He's staring straight at me.

CHAPTER Thirty-Five

I zigzag my way through the skaters, making sure to pay attention and not knock anyone down. By the time I get to the exit, Jamie's not there anymore. I spot him standing by a pinball machine, digging in his pocket for some change.

Now's my chance to talk to him. He's standing there. All by himself.

But I can't get my legs to move.

I watch as he drops the coins in the slot and starts to play.

Now what do I do? What if I'm making a big deal out of nothing? What if he stole those posters because he's just a thief? What if all those bruises are just because he's clumsy? What if I'm just being stupid?

I don't want to do this. But if I don't, I'll keep thinking about the stolen posters and the way he acted at the dinner. I want to get to the bottom of it so I can think of Jamie as being cute, not as being a jerk.

I make my way over to him. My skates don't make any sound on the carpet so he doesn't hear me coming. When I poke, poke, poke him on the shoulder he jumps and turns.

"Jeez! Did you have to sneak up on me like that?" he asks when he sees it's me.

"I didn't sneak up," I say. "Your back was turned. How else was I supposed to get your attention?"

"How about 'Hey, Jamie'?"

I shrug. And—because I have even less control of my tics when I'm nervous—I reach out to touch his shoulder.

Jamie narrows his eyes. I pull my hand back. Hold it against my mouth and swallow the grunt that's begging to come out.

"What exactly is your problem, anyway?" he asks.

"Funny, I was going to ask you the same thing."

I can't believe I just said that. I bite my lower lip. Wait for him to yell at me. Tell me I'm weird.

He drops his eyes. Looks away.

I hug my waist with my arms, grab onto my shirt with my hands and hold on tight. Maybe that will keep them from reaching out to touch him. Or worse, from touching the ground and turning it into a cartwheel! Not only would that look totally stupid but it would be pretty darn hard to do in skates.

After what seems like forever, he looks back at me. He takes a deep breath and blows it out. Shakes his head, looks down. Eyes focused on the floor, he asks, "You saw me take those posters, didn't you?"

I'm so surprised that anything I might have said gets stuck in my throat.

He lifts his head. "Well, did you or didn't you?"

"Just the one from Mrs. Morgan's class," I

finally get out. "But I figured it was you who took the others."

Jamie folds his arms in front of him, narrows his eyes. "Why didn't you tell on me?"

I shrug.

"That's not an answer."

"I didn't think it was that big a deal."

Jamie's eyes widen. "You sure act like it was."

Now I'm surprised. "How do you mean?"

"Why are you always staring at me in class and when I run by the softball field?"

He noticed me staring at softball practice! Embarrassed, I roll my skates back and forth on the rug, my lips clamped shut. I'm not sure what to say. Tell him that I can't let anything go until I have an answer? I don't think so. Then he'd want to know why. I don't want to tell him. I don't want him to think of me as that crazy girl with Tourette's.

I want to walk away. But if I leave, I'm just going to have to face him later. The questions won't go away until I have answers.

"So how'd you get that bruise on your side? And the black eye?" The words slip out of my mouth before I can stop them.

Jamie's face turns a bright red. "That's none of your business." He starts to walk away.

"Wait!" I call after him. But he keeps walking. I skate up to him, grab his arm. "Stop. Please. Can we just talk?"

He looks down at my hand, which is still holding onto him. I pull it away. Fist my hands at my side.

"So talk," he says.

I look around. We're standing close to the rink with its flashing lights and loud music. And people.

Lots of people going round and round.

"Not here," I say. "There are benches outside. How about there?"

He doesn't answer. Just turns and heads for the door.

I follow him, still not at all sure what I'm going to say.

CHAPTER Thirty-Six

We find a bench that's sitting in the shadow of the building, out of the hot sun. I sit on one end. Jamie sits on the other—and looks everywhere but at me. I roll my feet back and forth on the hard pavement. I like the sound it makes. Besides, the noise helps fill the silence.

I suppose I should start talking, since it was my idea to come out here. But I have no idea what to say or where to begin.

Uh. Oh.

I swallow hard, but I can't stop it. A grunt tickles deep in my throat and explodes out of my mouth.

Jamie jerks his head toward me. "What are you so mad about?"

"I'm not mad!" Grunt. Tap, tap, tap.

"Yeah. Right. You just make those weird sounds all the time for nothing."

Oh my god. Is that what he thinks? That I'm angry all the time?

I hold my body tight and rock back and forth. Out of the corner of my eye, I watch as Jamie stares at me, looks away, turns back, and stares again. My stomach tightens, and I feel like I'm going to throw up.

After a very long minute he stands. "If you're not going to talk, I'm leaving." He starts to walk away.

"Wait!"

Jamie stops. Turns toward me, hands on hips. "Now what?"

"I—I have something to tell you." Better he knows about the Tourette's then think I'm some kind of weird, angry person. I bend down and touch the ground. This time I don't hide it by messing with my laces. When I sit back up, I let out the grunt that's built up. I don't try and stop that either.

Jamie stands there, eyes narrowed, watching me.

I touch the ground. Tap, tap, tap on the bench. "It gets worse when I'm nervous." Grunt. I fight back tears. This is so hard.

"What gets worse? And what are you doing?"

"Please sit down." Grunt. "It's not easy to have this conversation with you standing over me like that."

Jamie sits on the bench, leaning as far away from me as he can.

I sigh. "I don't bite or anything." Tap. Tap. Tap.

He shrugs but sits up just a little bit straighter. He folds his arms in front of him. "I'm listening," he says.

I turn away from him and face forward. I don't want to look at him while I tell him my secret. I'm afraid of what I'll see.

Holding my hands tight in my lap, I take a breath

and start talking. "I have a neurological disorder. It's called Tourette Syndrome. The noises and touching and stuff—they're all a part of it. I can't stop them." Grunt. "My brain misfires sometimes. Makes me feel like I have to do those things. If I don't, well, it's like telling yourself not to breathe. You can put it off for so long, but eventually you can't not breathe."

I peek over at Jamie. He's sitting up now, and he's unfolded his arms. I take that as a good sign.

"So when I saw you steal the poster I thought that maybe, like me, there was a reason. Like you couldn't help yourself. Then I saw the bruise on your side and later you came to school with a black eye, and you acted so strange at the restaurant the other night, and I couldn't get all those things out of my mind, and I just had to ask you what's going on because—I just had to."

I'm out of breath and words by now. I sit there, staring ahead, waiting to see what Jamie will do. Does he think I'm weird? Will he walk away? I think I might explode if he doesn't say something soon.

But he just sits there, not moving or saying anything.

I can't help myself. I lean over and jab, jab, jab at his shoulder. He watches me, doesn't pull away. I start rocking back and forth again. Waiting him out. Hoping he understands.

"Okay," he finally says, "I get that you can't help the touching and grunting and all. But why do you have to know about the other stuff? I mean what's it to you if I have a black eye?"

I keep on rocking. This is so hard! People can see the tics. But they don't know what's going on in my head. Sometimes I don't even know.

"Izzy." That's the first time Jamie has called me by my name. He takes a deep breath. Looks up to the sky. "You—you don't have to tell me if you don't want to."

Tears form in my eyes. I don't want to cry, but I can't stop them from falling. I wipe them away with my sleeve, but they keep coming.

We sit there for a while, me sniffing back tears, Jamie looking out at the parking lot. Anywhere but at me.

"I think I know a little of what you're going through," he says at last. "I see the way people stare at my sister. It's hard on her, too."

"Oh. Poor Katie." I find a tissue in my pocket. Wipe my eyes and nose. "She seems so sweet."

"She is." He turns to me. "So like I said, you don't have to tell me anything more."

"No. I want to." I swipe at my eyes again. Chew on my lip. Decide to just say it. "I have OCD, too."

Jamie tilts his head, squishes his eyebrows together. "OCD? What's that?"

"It's short for Obsessive Compulsive Disorder."

Jamie looks totally confused. "I thought you said you had—what was it?"

"Tourette Syndrome. And you can have both."

He doesn't say anything, so I keep talking.

"OCD is a kind of like a brain tic. Sometimes a thought sticks in my head, and I can't get it out."

Jamie nods. "Okay. It kind of makes sense now. I wish you'd have said something sooner."

I stare down at the ground, stop myself from touching it. "It's not something I like to talk about."

"Yeah. I get that."

"You do?" I stare at him. Does he really mean it? "So, you don't think I'm weird or anything?"

Jamie sighs. "No. I don't think you're weird. I know things aren't always the way they look." He bites his lip. Nods like he's made up his mind. "Okay. I'll tell you about the posters and stuff, but you've got to promise me something first."

"What kind of promise?"

"That you'll keep everything I tell you to yourself. No sharing with best friends or anything."

That's more than fine with me. I put out my hand. "Deal."

We shake on it. Jamie sits there, not saying anything. I know exactly what he's going through. I squeeze my body tight to keep it still, and wait until he finds the words he is looking for.

Finally, he starts talking.

CHAPTER Thirty-Seven

"Have you ever done something really stupid?" Jamie says. "Something you're so ashamed of that you're glad nobody knows about it?"

I nod, though I don't think he wants an answer. He's not even looking at me.

"After I took that poster from Mrs. Morgan's room and found out how much it meant to her, I felt so guilty. I wanted to put it back, but my sister loved it so much I couldn't take it away from her."

"Wait. You took it for your sister?"

"Yeah. Mom took her out of the day care center she was in and started homeschooling her. I wanted to make the room feel more like school for her. So I took some posters. No big deal, right? They made her so happy, like she was a part of something normal."

I totally get that. "I bet if you told Mrs. Morgan, she would understand."

He shrugs. "I didn't want her to think I was a thief, which I guess I was."

"Is that why you didn't stay at the restaurant for your sister's birthday party? Because you thought I'd say something to your parents?"

He shrugs. "I told my mom the teachers gave me the posters. I guess they would have if I asked. But I didn't want to go through the whole explanation about Katie. I hate when people pity her. She's so cool. So smart. To me, she's just my little sister."

I tap, tap, tap him gently on the shoulder. "I wouldn't tell, Jamie. But I guess you didn't know that because you don't really know me."

Jamie mumbles something that sounds like "Yeah."

We sit quietly for a moment, but something still bugs me about it all. Something I can't let go. "What about all the bruises?"

He doesn't answer me.

"I told you everything about me," I say. "Everything. I trusted you, Jamie. Now you have to trust me."

"It's embarrassing," he says.

Frustrated, I grunt. Tap, tap, tap his shoulder. Bend over and touch the ground and grunt again. "Please don't talk to me about embarrassing. I've lived with it my whole life."

He looks my way. "I guess you do know." He hesitates then blurts out, "I got them trying to make Katie laugh."

"Why is that embarrassing?"

He shakes his head. "Because I'm a class-A klutz. I'm always messing up in team sports. The only reason I'm on track is because it doesn't take a lot of coordination. And I have stamina so I can do cross country races. I may not come in first, but I always finish. Plus, they're not picky. They need all the runners they can get."

"Sounds a little like our softball team."

Jamie smiles at that. "Yeah. I noticed you didn't have a deep bench."

He noticed that we don't have a lot of players? He actually noticed? I file that away to think about later and turn my attention back to the conversation.

"So the bruise on your side and the black eye?" I ask.

"It was so stupid. I was riding my bike, and Katie was sitting on the porch in her chair. I shouted to her to watch. 'I'll do a wheelie for you.' But I fell and caught my side on the handles bars."

I don't say anything. Afraid if I do he'll stop talking.

Jamie looks up at me. "I told you it was stupid."

I reach over and gently touch his shoulder, only once this time. "I don't think it's stupid. If I had a sister or brother, I hope they would feel the same way about me." Of course, I have to know it all. "What about the black eye?"

Jamie looks away. I wait. Give him some time and space.

"Sometimes my sister can't control her movements. Sometimes her arms jerk and lash out. I was sitting by her, and her fist hit me in the eye. I don't like to talk about it because it makes her feel bad."

"Poor Katie," I say.

"I don't think she'd want you to feel sorry for her. She's a great kid. Really smart, though some people just assume she's dumb because of the way she looks and acts."

"Wow. Do I understand that!"

Jamie looks at me like maybe for the first time he really sees me. "I guess you do."

I smile and grunt at the same time, which must look really strange, but I don't care. I feel free. Sharing secrets can do that, I guess.

"Jamie." He looks at me. "Thanks for telling me. I promise I won't say anything."

"Same here." He puts his hand out, and I shake it.

I drop his hand quickly, not sure about the tingling feeling that's working its way up my body. I tap, tap, tap the bench. Bend over and play with my laces.

"Something wrong?" he asks.

I shake my head. The words "I love you, Jamie" tickle my tongue. I bite my lip until it hurts. I will not say them. Not. Not. Not.

"Hey, Izzy!" It's Abbie, calling from the door of the building. I am so happy to see her, I jump up and skate over to her.

"I was looking all over for you." She stares at Jamie who's standing next to the bench. "Why are the two of you out here?"

"We're just talking," I say. "In fact, we were just about to come in. I'm starving."

Abbie glides over to Jamie. "Glad you could come." She glances down at his shoes. "Aren't you going to skate?"

Jamie shrugs. "I'm kind of a klutz, as you might have noticed." He points to his eye. It's almost totally healed, but it still has a little yellow bruising left. He's acting like it was his fault. Protecting his sister. He smiles and glances my way. "But I guess I'll give it a try."

I tap, tap, tap him on the shoulder. This time he doesn't pull away. Again that tingle starts at my toes and works its way up my body. And it has nothing to do with a tic.

"Great!" Abbie says. "Now come and eat before there's no food left."

Abbie grabs my hand and pulls me toward the door. "I want all the details," she whispers to me.

I glance at Jamie, trailing behind us. Not this time, Abbie. I have a promise to keep.

CHAPTER Thirty-Eight

A week passes. Jamie's been really nice to me ever since the party, even though some of the boys tease him about it, saying, "Jamie's got a girlfriend."

I don't know for sure if he feels that way about me. Like a girlfriend, I mean. Abbie said she'd find out. As far as I'm concerned, he's the cutest—and the nicest—guy in school. He did invite me to come over and meet Katie. He said she could use some friends. I like that idea. A lot.

The talk with Jamie also helped me make up my mind about something else. I don't have the courage yet to tell everyone about my Tourette's, but I want to tell my softball team. They deserve to know.

So here I am, standing in front of them. And I'm more nervous than I was the first time I took the field.

"Everyone take a seat," Coach says. We're in the dugout getting ready for practice. "Izzy has something she wants to tell you."

It's a hot, sticky afternoon. I wipe nervous sweat from my face with my sleeve, turn a grunt into a cough. Everyone is staring, waiting. I look at Abbie and Hannah. Hannah smiles her encouragement, and Abbie points two fingers at me, then at her eyes, her sign for "stay calm and look at me if you need to."

I clear my throat, punch, punch, punch my glove and stop myself just in time from reaching down to touch the ground.

I look over at Abbie and pretend I'm talking just to her. "I wanted to tell all of you that I have—" I hesitate. This is harder than I thought. I look down, take a breath and start over. "I have a disorder called Tourette Syndrome. Those things you see me do—like the tapping and the grunting—I don't want to do them. I'd stop if I could, but my body doesn't always listen to me."

"I don't get it," Ashley says. "How can your body do something you don't want it to do?"

"That a good question," I say. "Maybe this will help you understand. Everybody, try to not blink for a whole minute."

I watch as each of them hold their eyes wide open. Some look all around, struggling not to close their eyes. But, no matter how hard they try, they can't stop themselves.

"Wow," Ashley says. "That's really hard. I didn't last 10 seconds."

"Yeah"—I tap, tap, tap Ashley on the shoulder— "That's kind of what I go through most of the time."

After that, I get tons of questions from my teammates. I answer them as best I can.

I don't tell them about the OCD stuff. It was hard enough talking about Tourette's. Funny thing is that OCD helps me with softball. I'm kind of obsessed with hitting the ball over the fence so I've been spending a lot of time in the batting cage practicing. Even Coach noticed my swing is better.

After the talk, most of the girls come up to me and thank me for telling them. Even Meghan.

"I wish you'd have said something sooner," she says. "I thought you were just goofing off in the field. By the way, you're doing a lot better out there."

I smile and nod. Sometimes people can surprise you.

"Thanks, Izzy, for sharing that with us," Coach says. "We all have problems to overcome. Some of them more visible like yours. Some not so much."

I'd never thought about any of that before. There are probably a lot of people out there with problems. We just don't always see them.

"Okay, everyone. Warm-up time," Coach says.

I actually like doing the stretches and jumping jacks now, and I've discovered I'm a fast runner. Even though I still touch the ground once in a while, I can keep up with everybody while we race around the field.

I feel happy and focused. Now that I don't have to hide my tics anymore, I'm hoping I'll do them less often.

We take the field, and Coach starts us off with batting practice.

I'm last at bat, and Meghan is on the mound. She's one of our fastest pitchers. At first, I mostly hit infield grounders, but as I get used to her speed I start hitting past the short stop or second baseman and into the outfield.

Meghan sets for another pitch.

I take a deep breath, let it out slowly, and focus. I watch closely as she does her wind-up. I see her release the ball. And I time it perfectly.

Crack! Just from the sound of it I know. This ball is not a grounder. This ball is flying, flying.

Over the second baseman's head.

Between the center and right fielders.

Over the fence!

"Oh. My. God. I hit a home run ball. I hit a home run ball."

There are a lot of "way to go" shouts from the team. Even Meghan calls out, "Nice hit." Me? I'm doing a happy dance.

Coach comes over, all smiles. "I knew you had it in you." She tap, tap, taps me gently on the shoulder. "I think we'll end batting practice with that one. Time for drills."

I high five Abbie on my way to right field. As I trot to my position, I spot Jamie standing by the fence. He has a softball in his hand. The softball I just slammed over the fence.

"Nice hit," he says.

I smile. Punch, punch, punch the sweet spot of my glove.

He smiles back, tosses the ball to me, and starts running toward the disappearing backs of his track team.

Jamie saw the homerun hit! And he waited for me! I do another happy dance.

"Palmer!" Coach calls to me. "Keep your head in the game."

"Yes, ma'am," I say, but I can't stop the sound that comes out of my mouth. It's more of a whoop than a grunt.

I'm standing in right field, watching as Coach hits a grounder to the third baseman who throws it to first. Her throw is high and it sails over Abbie's head. But I'm there, backing her up, just like a right fielder's supposed to.

Everybody misses a ball now and then. But it's nice to know that there are people there, backing you up. Even people like me.

Maybe, just maybe, I'm not so different after all.

About Janet McLaughlin

Janet McLaughlin has been involved in the communication field most of her adult life as a writer, editor, and teacher. Her love of mysteries and the mystical are evident in her novels. She is a member of the Society of Children's Book Writers and Illustrators and the Florida Writers Association. She lives in Florida with her husband, Tom, and along with her writing, enjoys playing tennis, walking, traveling, and meeting people.

Did you enjoy this book?

Please consider leaving a brief review online for *Different* and the Soul Sight Mysteries: *Haunted Echo* and *Fireworks*.

Would you like to know about the latest Absolute Love Publishing releases? Join our newsletter on our website home page: absolutelovepublishing. com.

About
Absolute Love Publishing

Absolute Love Publishing is an independent book publisher devoted to creating and publishing books that promote goodness in the world.

www.AbsoluteLovePublishing.com

Books by
Absolute Love Publishing

Young Adult and Children's Books

Dear One, Be Kind by Jennifer Farnham
This beautiful children's book takes young children on a journey of harmony and empathy. Using rhyme and age-appropriate language and imagery, *Dear One, Be Kind* illustrates how children can embrace feelings of kindness and love for everyone they meet, even when others are seemingly hurtful. By revealing the unseen message behind common childhood experiences, the concept of empathy is introduced, along with a gentle knowledge of our interconnectedness and the belief that, through kindness, children have the power to change their world. Magically illustrated with a soothing and positive message, this book is a joy for children and parents alike!

Different by Janet McLaughlin
Twelve-year-old Izzy wants to be like everyone else, but she has a secret. She isn't weird or angry, like some of the kids at school think. Izzy has Tourette syndrome. Hiding outbursts and tics from her classmates is hard enough, but when a new girl arrives, Izzy's fear of losing her best friend makes Izzy's symptoms worse. And when she sees her crush act suspiciously, runaway thoughts take root inside of her. As the pressure builds and her world threatens to spin out of control, Izzy must

face her fear and reveal her secret, whatever the costs.

Authentic and perceptive, *Different* shines a light on the delicate line of a child's hopes and fears and inspires us all to believe that perhaps we are not so different after all.

The Adima Chronicles by Steve Schatz

Adima Rising

For millennia, the evil Kroledutz have fed on the essence of humans and clashed in secret with the Adima, the light weavers of the universe. Now, with the balance of power shifting toward darkness, time is running out. Guided by a timeless Native American spirit, four teenagers from a small New Mexico town discover they have one month to awaken their inner power and save the world.

Rory, Tima, Billy, and James must solve four ancient challenges by the next full moon to awaken a mystical portal and become Adima. If they fail, the last threads of light will dissolve, and the universe will be lost forever. Can they put aside their fears and discover their true natures before it's too late?

Adima Returning

The Sacred Cliff is crumbling and with it the Adima way of life! Weakened by the absence of their beloved friend James, Rory, Tima, and Billy must battle time and unseen forces to unite the greatest powers of all dimensions in one goal.

They must move the Sacred Cliff before it traps all Adima on Earth—and apart from the primal energy of the Spheres—forever!

Aided by a surprising and timeless maiden, the three light-weaving teens travel across the planes of existence to gain help from the magical creatures who guard the Adima's most powerful objects, the Olohos. There is only one path to success: convince the guardians to help. Fail and the Cliff dissolves, destroying the once-eternal Spheres and the interdimensional light weavers known as Adima.

Like the exciting adventures of *Adima Rising*, the second spellbinding book of The Adima Chronicles, *Adima Returning*, will have your senses reeling right up until its across-worlds climax. Will conscious creation and the bonds of friendship be enough to fight off destructive forces and save the world once again?

Serafina Loves Science! by Cara Bartek, Ph.D.

Cosmic Conundrum

In *Cosmic Conundrum*, sixth grader Serafina Sterling finds herself accepted into the Ivy League of space adventures for commercial astronauts, where she'll study with Jeronimo Musgrave, a famous and flamboyant scientist who brought jet-engine minivans to the suburbs. Unfortunately, Serafina also meets Ida Hammer, a 12-year-old superstar of science who has her own theorem, a Nobel-Prize-winning mother, impeccable fashion sense—and a million social media followers. Basically, she's everything Serafina's not. Or so Serafina thinks.

Even in an anti-gravity chamber, Serafina realizes surviving junior astronaut training will take more than just a thorough understanding of Newton's Laws. She'll have to conquer her fear of public speaking, stick to the rules, and overcome the antics of Ida. How will Serafina survive this cosmic conundrum?

Quantum Quagmire
Serafina suspects something is wrong when her best friend, Tori Copper, loses interest in their most cherished hobbies: bug hunting and pizza nights. When she learns Tori's parents are getting a divorce and that Tori's mom is moving away, Serafina vows to discover a scientific solution to a very personal problem so that Tori can be happy again. But will the scientific method, a clever plan, and a small army of arachnids be enough to reunite Tori's parents? When the situation goes haywire, Serafina realizes she has overlooked the smallest, most quantum of details. Will love be the one challenge science can't solve?

Join Serafina in another endearing adventure in book two of the Serafina Loves Science! series.

The Soul Sight Mysteries by Janet McLaughlin

Haunted Echo

Sun, fun, toes in the sand, and daydreams about her boyfriend back home. That's what teen psychic Zoey Christopher expects for her spring break on an exotic island. But from the moment she steps foot onto her best friend Becca's property, Zoey realizes the island has other plans: chilling drum beats, a shadowy ghost, and a mysterious voodoo doll.

Zoey has always seen visions of the future, but when she arrives at St. Anthony's Island to vacation among the jet set, she has her first encounter with a bona fide ghost. Forced to uncover the secret behind the girl's untimely death, Zoey quickly realizes that trying to solve the case will thrust her into mortal danger—and into the arms of a budding crush. Can Zoey put the tormented spirit's soul to rest without her own wild emotions haunting her?

Fireworks

Dreams aren't real. Psychic teen Zoey Christopher knows the difference between dreams and visions better than anyone, but ever since she and her best friend returned from spring vacation, Zoey's dreams have been warning her that Becca is in danger. But a dream isn't a vision—right?

Besides, Zoey has other things to worry about,

like the new, cute boy in school. Dan obviously has something to hide, and he won't leave Zoey alone—even when it causes major problems with Josh, Zoey's boyfriend. Is it possible he knows her secret?

Then, one night, Becca doesn't answer any of Zoey's texts or calls. She doesn't answer the next morning either. When Zoey's worst fears come true, her only choice is to turn to Dan, whom she discovers has a gift different from her own but just as powerful. Is it fate? Will using their gifts together help them save Becca, or will the darkness win? Discover what's real and what's just a dream in *Fireworks*, book two of the Soul Sight Mysteries!

Connect with us and learn more about our books and upcoming releases at AbsoluteLovePublishing.com.

26960355R00098

Made in the USA
Columbia, SC
21 September 2018